He was tot

She wanted som
who cared. Rick ~~~~~~~~ ~~~~~ used her
for his own pur~~~~~~~~~, callously manipulating
her emotions until she felt like a puppet, with
him holding all the strings.

'What's the matter, Helen? Upset because you
got the wrong Frazer? James would suit you.
You could both live in that polite never-never
land where nothing nasty ever happens.'

Dear Reader

Wouldn't it be wonderful to drop everything and jet off to Australia—the land of surf, sunshine, 'barbies' and, of course, the vast, untamed Outback? Mills & Boon contemporary romances offer you that very chance! Tender and exciting love stories by favourite Australian authors bring vividly to life the city, beach and bush, and introduce you to the most gorgeous heroes that Down Under has to offer...check out your local shops, or with our Readers' Service, for a trip of a lifetime!

The Editor

Christine Greig works full-time as a senior marketing manager in the communications industry. This involves a great deal of travel, both within Europe and the United States, which she enjoys very much. She has a BA Hons degree and a diploma in marketing. She is in her thirties, came originally from North Yorkshire, England, and is married.

Recent titles by the same author:

THE PARIS TYPE

STRONG MAGIC

BY

CHRISTINE GREIG

MILLS & BOON LIMITED
ETON HOUSE   18-24 PARADISE ROAD
RICHMOND   SURREY   TW9 1SR

*First published in Great Britain 1992
by Mills & Boon Limited*

© Christine Greig 1992

*Australian copyright 1992
Philippine copyright 1992
This edition 1992*

ISBN 0 263 77578 X

*Set in Times Roman 10 on 11 pt.
01-9206-58994 C*

Made and printed in Great Britain

CHAPTER ONE

HELEN HOWARD blinked as the blurred lights of a passing train briefly lit up the railway carriage and then rattled past, the long summer evenings that made June so delightful cruelly shortened that night by a dark belt of cloud that spattered intermittent rain against the windows.

Helen wouldn't have noticed the scenery much anyway. She had a lot to think about. Her mother's response to her plans to live on the Hebridean island of Cladach had shocked her. She had been surprised to find herself the major beneficiary of Fiona MacSween's will. She had always assumed her mother, the old lady's niece, would be Aunt Fi's legatee. Visiting Cladach had been an act of respect; she hadn't expected it to make such a strong impact upon her.

Helen had returned from her visit to the island to the house in Hampstead in the late evening, to find a note telling her that her parent was playing bridge and that she would find her supper in the microwave. Consequently they hadn't spoken until the next morning. Waking, Helen had listened to the swish of traffic and car doors banging. She had been surprised at the deep pang of longing she had felt for the sound of the wind fresh from the sea and the call of gulls screaming their joy over Cladach Bagh.

The low drone of the radio chattering incessantly had witnessed her mother's need for constant noise, and Helen had joined her at the breakfast table, suddenly aware of how different they were. Not that she had loved her mother any less; it was just that they weren't alike and that was something that had never occurred to her before. It had become clear that Moira Howard had taken her quick return as confirmation of her opinion that Helen would be bored to tears in a week. She had received the news of Helen's return to Cladach with horror.

'You can't mean it!' She had paled visibly. 'But what about your career? There's nothing there, Helen! It's professional suicide!'

'My career is over.' Helen had refused to dwell on the subject. She had pulled out of the race for the anchor role in a projected consumer programme when the producer, Michael Burton, had added several unwritten clauses to the contract.

'But Mr Burton's been on the phone several times——'

'I won't change my mind.' Helen was stubborn. 'I've decided to spend some time on Cladach. It's different,' she attempted to explain. 'I didn't open the shop and they were queuing up outside. I felt necessary.' Her green eyes shone, making Moira Howard shake her head uncomprehendingly.

'Your grandmother was right. She told me to keep you away from Cladach. Aunt Fiona was always trying to get you there and now she's won!'

'I thought you liked her!' Helen was astonished at the amount of bitterness in her mother's tone.

'That's not the point.' She subsided then as if realising she was becoming irrational. 'Oh, I don't know, it's all such a long time ago, and I suppose there must have been faults on both sides. But she was my mother and I can't help thinking you're betraying her.'

Moira Howard had taken some persuading, but eventually the story had come out. There had indeed been a reason why Helen's grandmother had left Cladach. Her story was not a new one. Clara MacSween had been young, pretty and restless with island life. She had caught the attention of the laird and, flattered by his interest, she had quickly fancied herself in love with him. Influenza had carried off the girls' parents when Clara was just fifteen, and Fiona had been too busy with the shop to watch her younger sister properly. It was well known that Malcolm Frazer had married his wife, a McKinnon, to gain entrance to the aristocracy and that there was little love in the match, the McKinnons needing Frazer's money. He had kept his infidelities away from the island and it had seemed that the relationship with Clara hadn't gone beyond flirtation. Certainly Helen's grandmother had insisted it was nothing more.

The people of Cladach had taken the matter more seriously; devoutly Roman Catholic, they had shunned Clara until it had become unbearable and she'd been forced to leave. Fiona had travelled with her sister to London and seen her settled, but she had been unable to make England her home. Clara MacSween had sworn never to go back to the island and had insisted her daughter refuse Fiona's invitations.

'Cladach belongs in the Dark Ages,' Moira Howard had insisted. 'I know something has happened to upset you, but you're in a hard business. You've got to bounce back, not run away.'

Helen thought back over her mother's words, but the idea of returning to TV journalism made her shudder. At the moment the 'Dark Ages' on Cladach seemed infinitely preferable. If she had needed anything to convince her the constant buzz of the telephone from the Press, and the photographer a policeman had had to remove from the garden would have sufficed. Her mother's view that it was a healthy sign of public interest made Helen think that Moira Howard would be better suited to media manipulation than she was. She had always abhorred that side of the business.

The conductor passing down the aisle brought her attention back to the present. The train journey had taken

most of the day and Helen's aching muscles were badly
in need of some exercise. She eased her neck, her perfectly groomed hair persistently regaining order despite
her restless movements. Give it a month, she reflected,
and her blonde locks would be wild and windswept. The
prospect didn't bother her a great deal—she would have
to be firm with the brush.

'Get the feeling you should have chosen some other
form of transport?' A transatlantic accent with an
underlying rhythm that suggested a Scottish origin in-
truded on her privacy, and Helen's delicately cut features froze into a polite mask.

'Don't tell me. You don't want to talk and you object
to strange men chatting you up.'

Apart from his initial perception, he didn't take a blind
bit of notice of Helen's lack of response. Easing himself
down beside her, the man awaited her annoyed glance
with a smile that held a teasing warmth that was wickedly
familiar.

'If it's entertainment you want, you've picked on the
wrong person.' Her voice was cool, emerald-green eyes
hard with rejection. 'I shan't hesitate to call the guard.'

Regarding her with mock-solemnity, he remained
totally uncrushed. 'Where are you going? You look mis-
erable. Boyfriend trouble?'

Helen counted to ten, ready to let fly with a blistering
attack on chauvinistic males who thought any woman
alone was waiting for company. Then she recognised him.
The words died in her throat and the irony of the situation almost made her laugh. She was sitting next to the
'man most wanted' as far as the media were concerned,
with the chance to ask all the questions they were dying
to know. Strangely all Helen could think of to say was,
'I'm sure there are a lot of people who'd be only too
pleased to talk to you.'

'Oh.' He frowned, and Helen received the impression
that he was about to move off. How he expected anon-

ymity, when his face was on the front of nearly every daily, she failed to understand. She supposed she should feel grateful to him—he had relegated her to the gossip column.

'You're not a lady of the Press, are you?' Black brows drew together into a frown, then he laughed drily. 'But then, you wouldn't tell me if you were.'

'Don't let me detain you,' she offered sweetly, shrinking at the thought of the publicity if they were discovered sitting next to each other on the train.

'This could be reverse psychology.' He studied her in a way she found decidedly unsettling.

'I'm not that sophisticated.'

'OK.' He smiled again, a row of perfect teeth, living proof that he had a sense of humour. 'Rick Cameron.' He held out his hand.

'I know.' She ignored the gesture of friendship and he whistled between his teeth.

'If you're not careful I'm going to think you don't like me.'

Helen tried to keep her mouth level but she couldn't help the smile that tugged at her lips. She wouldn't be human if she hadn't felt the smallest stab of curiosity. She was sitting next to a mega-star who had upset his latest leading lady by disappearing from the film set, leaving the volatile Vi Channing to spend her first days on the set watching the minor characters film their scenes first. The ensuing rumbles from the studio had quickly found their way to the ears of the Press, and speculation was high. Where had the handsome, eminently eligible Mr Cameron gone and, more to the point, with whom?

Rick Cameron was one of the new breed of film moguls who had a finger in every pie. He owned his own company, produced and directed some of the best box-office hits, retaining his own artistic credibility by being choosy about his scripts. He was a handsome man, and it was all too easy with his looks to become typecast as 'the hero' and not get the chance to do anything else. He had taken to accepting offers in low-budget films if the part was interesting and only took on the big money-spinners if they allowed him to expand his talents. Helen rated him quite highly as an actor but, with her present disenchantment with the world of entertainment and men in general, she couldn't help a measure of reserve.

'I'll forget about your boyfriend. You forget about the film.' He offered a deal and Helen softened, despite her earlier qualms.

Perhaps they had a story in common. He looked tired behind the easy charm, and at least she knew who he was. She wondered if he had chosen to travel by train to avoid publicity. Helen had certainly done that—there were nearly always photographers at Heathrow.

'I'm not sure I'll make a very good conversationalist,' she admitted quietly. 'I've got a lot on my mind.'

Rick Cameron nodded and gave her a conspiratorial wink. 'We'll protect each other, then.'

Folding his arms across his chest, he tilted his head back against the chair rest and closed his eyes. Helen was rather taken aback at this abrupt cessation of speech and then, realising it wasn't a pose, she slowly began to relax.

Glancing around furtively, Helen viewed their immediate neighbours. A fat, balding man sat behind a newspaper across the aisle. There were several miniatures of gin littering the table and she guessed by the droop of the paper that he was unlikely to pay them much attention. Other than that, the other inhabitants of the carriage were some distance away.

Studying Rick Cameron, she tried to disassociate him from his screen image. It was no good: he was eye-catching. His tall, muscular build, the Californian tan and that peculiar sense of presence emanating from him were barely subdued by the casual clothes he wore. Early to mid-thirties, she catalogued... The clinical appraisal broke down, much to her discomfort. He was very good-looking! From her close proximity she could see the dark little spikes of bristle shadowing his jaw and the dark brown hair that forked attractively over his collar. His eyes, she knew, were hazel. Sometimes in his films they had seemed a brilliant blue, and other times as dark as night. Dark, well-shaped eyebrows were above a nose that had been straight, but a break at the bridge had taken away the chocolate-box quality to his looks and enhanced their masculinity. His mouth was firm, his chin slightly clefted; he certainly didn't owe much to artifice or the smile of the camera.

She should move while he was asleep, she told herself. They were like spotlights, emphasising the other where one might have escaped notice. The fat man got up as the train slowed and she sank back into her chair. No one else got on and the train moved off again, leaving them undiscovered. Deciding a move might attract more attention than their secluded spot, she looked out into the fading light and tried to put together the reason for being on that train—for changing her life. She had really wanted the job as an investigative journalist for consumer affairs. The disappointment had bitten deep when she had discovered that her credentials as a journalist and presenter weren't enough to secure the post. Was she running away? Was she a coward? The accusation had underscored her mother's advice to take the knocks and get back on her feet again. But the disillusionment wasn't a moment's affair. It had started back at the beginning. Her green eyes took on the colour of troubled seas, remembering the hurt she had felt when her first break in television had been accompanied by revelations of her romance with an out-of-work actor called Gary Chambers. The relationship hadn't progressed beyond the holding hands and kissing stage, but the rag that had publicised the piece had concentrated on her immaturity in a way that had made her sound abnormal.

Looking back, she knew her success had been too immediate. She had been doing 'on the spot' interviews for Metro TV since she was nineteen. Gary Chambers's desire to make some easy money had made her wary of men, and no one had been allowed close since. Not that they hadn't tried, some more persistently than others. Helen had known that Michael Burton was attracted to her. Had she flirted with him to secure the job she wanted? Had she let him think there would be unseen gains in preferring her to the other candidates? It was impossible to tell. Being friendly was part of the business, part of the game. It was when the game had become real that Helen had decided to pull out. She knew there'd be others without her scruples, but she couldn't live with the idea of selling herself that way. Michael Burton could seek elsewhere for his mistress! She had a moment's satisfaction imagining the embarrassing questions being asked by the media. Her fan mail, built up during her work on the holiday programme *Chase the Sun*, reflected her popularity, and the lack of gossip attached to her name brought both admiration and curiosity. The newspapers loved a mystery, especially when they were free to invent whatever scenario they liked. They would stay on the right side of the libel laws, but sooner or later someone would hint at pressure from on high and Michael Burton would have a hard time explaining that away to his rich and very possessive wife.

Before she had known about the cottage on Cladach she had been twenty-five, looking at the ashes of her career. Now she laid such bitter thoughts aside. On Cladach she would try to solve that conundrum of life, how much could be sacrificed before the indefinable riches of self-respect were gone forever.

The garbled message over the tannoy system announced something about the buffet closing, and Helen realised she was thirsty.

Rising, she tried to move past Rick Cameron without waking him.

'Coffee, black,' he muttered without appearing to wake.

'Sorry?' She thought for a moment she was hearing things.

'Coffee, black, please,' he restated his preference. His dark lashes frayed open to study her sleepily. 'I can't go—there's a bunch of kids hanging about near the counter.'

'Oh.' She didn't like the sound of that.

'They won't bother you.' He clearly misinterpreted her concern. 'They just might want autographs and then they'll be sitting behind us, giggling. Girls,' he offered as if this completed the explanation.

'Naturally.' She was rather tart.

'Quite natural,' he agreed. 'But it gets to be a pain after a while.' Regarding her with curiosity, he clearly wondered what she was waiting for. When his gaze became a touch more personal she found herself moving out into the aisle, and felt unaccountably hot.

'What's the matter with me?' she muttered. 'He's only a man.' But a very attractive one, a rebel voice argued in her head. That sort of complication she didn't need!

The buffet compartment was thankfully empty when she purchased a coffee for Rick Cameron and a cool drink for herself. Upon her return she found that he had moved to the window-seat and was watching the distant lights of some small village getting closer.

'It's better if you're on the outside,' he offered as an explanation.

Viewing his long legs, she didn't think it was better for him, but he clearly was paranoid about being spotted. It was strange; sitting next to an international film star reduced her own tension, and she complied, handing him the polystyrene cup and sitting down, pouring her citrus drink into a plastic beaker.

'Here's to style.' He touched his beaker to hers. 'Where are you going...? I don't know your name.'

'Helen.'

'Nice.' He subjected her to a long appraisal. 'I guess you're sick of the line about launching a thousand ships.'

'Very.'

He grinned. 'You're smart. I like that. I've had my fill of hysterical bimbos.'

Helen felt rather put out without knowing why. When he talked she had the weird feeling that they had known each other for years rather than an hour, most of which he had spent in sleep. Perhaps it was the States or Hollywood that gave him that immediacy. She was used to the false camaraderie of the TV world, but it rarely had the same quality as Rick Cameron's approach.

'I'm visiting the Hebrides.' She was deliberately vague, and his smile had a mocking quality to it.

'All of them?'

'No, of course not.' She received the impression he was familiar with the area. 'How about you? Or is that a secret?'

'West coast.' His smirk suggested that he was willing to be as vague as she.

'I hope you have good weather,' she commented politely, willing that to be the end of the conversation.

'Sure. Weather's important,' he muttered, watching the fire stoke in the depths of her green eyes. 'Classic features, with cat's eyes...' he growled low in his throat. 'You'd interrupt any man's sleep.'

'Please don't let me spoil yours.' The familiarity had lost its charm and she picked up a magazine, deliberately closing him out.

'Reads easier the other way up,' he commented, turning his shoulder towards the window and hunching in the seat, prepared, it seemed, to follow her advice.

Irritated, she went red when she discovered the magazine was upside-down. Turning it round, she pretended to read it, but her mind returned to Cladach. The island was becoming the touchstone by which she measured everything else. Summing up the image of James Frazer, Cladach's laird, she thought how pleasant and civilised he was in comparison to the over-familiar, conceited oaf sitting next to her.

She had been surprised at the cordiality of her welcome. Helen had expected a certain degree of hostility. The weather had been atrocious in March when her aunt had died, and the Howards had been unable to attend her funeral.

'She'd want to be with her own people,' Moira Howard had reflected sadly. 'Some never come away and others never go back. It's strange, island life. You'd hate it. There are precious few shops there. What would you do without Oxford Street?' Helen had winced at that. It had made her sound superficial. She had met models who had a hotline to their hairdressers and laughed at their excesses. She wasn't like that. A smart appearance was essential in media presentation, but when she was off duty she was quite happy in a pair of jeans.

Recalling her first visit to Cladach, Helen reflected that Murdo Buchanan's fishing boat had certainly not demanded Paris fashions. She had dressed in a pale blue trouser suit and a windcheater, remaining warm and comfortable as the boat had lifted and fallen on the choppy sea. The memory of the brisk sea breeze brought a smile of pure pleasure to her troubled features. It had been a long journey; she had been travelling since early in the morning and still hadn't reached her destination by teatime. But it had been worth it, she recalled vividly; Cladach had been just what she had needed.

The day had begun with a flight from London to Glasgow and then on to Balivanich airport on Benbecula. It was one of those oddities of travel that, when a long journey from the south of England to the distant Outer Hebrides should take a matter of three to four hours,

the remaining distance to Cladach, the small island west
of Barra, should take nearly as long.

Helen hadn't minded. She had been glad of the sea
journey. Sometimes travel was too quick, and the mind
lagged behind the body in its ability to adapt. The intense pressures she had suffered needed time to dis-
sipate. She loved the sea, and it repaid her love by
calming her mind with its hypnotic motion.

Benbecula was midway between North and South Uist.
Helen had meticulously planned her journey so that the
bus ride across the bridge to the southern island and the
ferry to Barra completed the most economic time
package possible. It had once been her job to research
such things and she had consequently avoided the pit-
falls less seasoned travellers made when they assumed
island hopping would be a matter of hours rather than
days. It had been pure luck, though, to chance upon a
fisherman preparing to take supplies to Cladach.

The Outer Hebrides! The name set fire to the imagination. The principal islands were also called the Long
Island. Her mind had silently gone over the names. Lewis
and Harris, the Uists, Benbecula and Barra. She had
smiled as she'd remembered doing the same thing as a
child, chanting them with all the fervour of a mystical
invocation. How often she'd begged to be taken there,
but her enthusiasm had been frowned on.

The Long Island group had a reputation for being
bleak and riddled with sea lochs. Trees were virtually
non-existent, the soil poor, and, when land did manage
to gain dominance over water and peat bog, moorland
added to the wild, barren landscape. Helen wondered if
Cladach was largely infertile. Its name meant 'rocky
shore', which suggested it didn't deviate from the pattern
set by its neighbours, and she understood the number
living there to be very small.

She had caught the sideways glance of Murdo
Buchanan. He had been reluctantly impressed. He had
expected her to be seasick. City types usually were.

As she became aware of something of the man's
thoughts Helen's green eyes gleamed. She had travelled
the world both in luxury and on a shoestring for *Chase
the Sun*. A slight cloud passed over her countenance. It
would take more than the corrupt practices of a TV boss
or a choppy boat ride to quell her spirit. Helen's chin
lifted, her gaze fixed on the grey patch of rock getting
closer and closer until it distinguished itself into a cliff.

At first it seemed incredible that such a gentle soul as
Fiona MacSween should have lived on this rocky outpost
of the Western Isles. Aunt Fi, as Helen had called her
since her young tongue had first lisped over the name,
had seemed more suited to Brighton or Harrogate. But
the old lady had clearly thought otherwise. Despite the
Howards' many requests for her to make her home with
them in Hampstead, she had remained on Cladach until
her death.

The fishing boat attracted a noisy following that grew
as they neared the cliffs. Manx shearwaters, auks, gulls
and other birds Helen failed to recognise circled and
dived at them in raucous welcome. The cliffs were lit-
tered with seabirds, so many that the grey rock seethed
with a life of its own. Helen could hardly keep the smile
off her face. This was just what she needed. She wished
that she had made the journey when Aunt Fi was alive.
Remorse was cheap, she reminded herself, but the legacy
had made her aware of how much her aunt must have
wished to share her love for her home.

Sunshine broke through the cloud, gilding the white
froth on the waves. Tidal currents tugged at the small
craft, and the fisherman concentrated on steering
through the jagged outriders protecting Cladach Bagh.

'Looks as if I might make it here'n back in a day.' Her skipper tilted his head skywards. 'Sometimes Cladach's cut off for weeks.'

'Not in June, surely?' She had listened enough to Aunt Fi to know the run of the seasons. Murdo Buchanan was subtly denying the charm of a fine day. This is a rough place and not for romantic Sassenachs, was the message coming through loud and clear.

'You'd be surprised.' He eyed her curiously. The men on Cladach would be getting out their Sunday best, he suspected. He disapproved of women in trousers, but thought this young lassie, if she had a mind to it, would look good in a sack.

As the boat came into sight of the shore Helen was surprised to see a group of people standing on a slab of rock that formed a natural jetty. There seemed to be quite a crowd—over thirty, she guessed. So much for her mother's dozen.

'*Feasgar math dhuibh, Murdo.*' Cries of greeting mingled with the gull squawk.

Murdo Buchanan replied in Gaelic, and Helen could tell he was talking about her. It seemed she was expected. No one expressed surprise.

'Good day, Miss Howard.' A cultured voice, barely accented, caught her attention.

A man stood, heavily supported by sturdy sticks. He had reddish fair hair and pale blue eyes. Whatever his infirmity, he suffered pain. Lines revealing the fact were etched deeply around his mouth and forehead.

'Let me welcome you to our small island. My name is James Frazer. We could pretend we're after post and provisions from the mainland, but there's a fair dash of curiosity when a stranger comes to Cladach.'

It was a long greeting, especially when the boat was busily trying to smash itself against the jetty and Murdo was grunting and shouting orders to those helping to tie up. James Frazer was a man who felt confident of holding attention. Despite his present condition, he had an authoritative presence.

'I'm pleased to meet you... everyone.' She remembered the others, having disembarked with more clumsiness than elegance and being grasped warmly by the hand by the laird. James Frazer's official title had been whispered by Murdo, and his tone had suggested that she was being personally honoured by the welcome. 'My great-aunt loved Cladach; I'm sure I shall too.'

She would have been a fool if she hadn't seen the doubt in the predominantly blue eyes around her. Helen wasn't sure why she'd said such a thing other than out of politeness. It had never occurred to her that she might want to keep the cottage. She had meant to holiday there. Stay for a while and think about the future. Find a space to heal in and then plan a new direction. Stay on Cladach? The idea had seemed preposterous. She would be bored silly in a week. Wouldn't she?

A Land Rover stood waiting, and James Frazer indicated it with a gallant wave that his stick spoilt slightly. Helen thought it added to the charm of the gesture and she thanked him with warmth. She had wondered how she'd find Aunt Fi's cottage, having received only the barest details from the solicitor.

'Cathy Ferguson's been running the shop for your aunt for the last few years.' James climbed into the back of the vehicle beside her, a young man he referred to as Andy taking the wheel. 'I'm sure you'll find everything is in order.'

Helen was startled, and it showed. She had thought the business sold. When she saw the cottage she realised the impracticality of that. Cottage and shop were one. It wasn't far from the bay, on a thin, winding road with another cottage viewable at a distance of about a mile. That wasn't the only shock. The cottage had a cow in the field behind, and a garden beyond that stretched as far as she could see and was mostly given over to vegetables.

'The children have worked the croft.' James Frazer was clearly amused. 'It's good practice for them. It meant your aunt had her vegetables and milk and they got pocket money from the surplus. They're eager to know about any renegotiations you might care to make.'

Helen laughed, her cheeks flushing attractively with bewilderment. 'I had no idea,' she admitted truthfully. 'I...' She just shook her head. A cottage, a croft, not to mention the cow... Her cheeks reddened again with shame. These people had helped Aunt Fi. They were far more her heirs than some stranger from Hampstead.

'I never knew,' she admitted to herself, unaware of her words being audible.

James Frazer wore a rather bleak expression for a moment that suggested that she had triggered off some thought, deeply personal.

'We look after our own here.' His smile was quick and comforting. 'It's the way of life on Cladach. No one thinks of it as charity. Your aunt did her service to the community while she could; she was repaid in kind. She talked of you often, though.' He lowered his voice confidentially in an imitation of Aunt Fi imparting a secret. '"Helen's not like her mother. She's not suited to city life."'

The comment struck her with all the force of a thunderbolt. Had Aunt Fi really thought that? But how could she? TV journalism was about as cosmopolitan as you could get. And yet you weren't happy, a little voice piped up inside her. Maybe Aunt Fi had been right!

Cathy Ferguson came to the cottage door when the Land Rover pulled up outside. James Frazer apologised for not getting out of the vehicle, a light slap at his legs indicating the reason why.

'Samhrad Taigh,' he nodded at the cottage. 'The Summer House. It's well named.' His glance touched Cathy for a moment, but the girl had turned to Helen.

'Welcome to Cladach.' She extended her hand.

'Thank you.' Helen didn't know what else to say; she was in shock.

'You'll be welcome at Castealcreag when you've settled in. I'll be in touch.' James Frazer shouted the invitation over the power of the engine.

They both waved goodbye to the two men and then Cathy stood back to allow Helen to enter Aunt Fi's home.

The cottage, besides the shop area, consisted of a parlour, bedroom, kitchen and bathroom. The parlour was indeed a shrine to summer. It combined an elderly woman's attachment to chintz with a love of light and flowers that the long Hebridean winter could turn into far-off memory. A carpet, the colour of dry sage, was lightened by faded Axminster rugs. Dominating the room, a chintz couch loaded with cushions was flanked by armchairs, served by strategically placed occasional tables in bamboo and walnut. Potted plants and cut flowers refreshed the eye and scented the air. It was delightful. Helen wanted to turn to Aunt Fi and ask a million questions.

'I never really knew you,' she whispered silently. 'But you knew me.'

Tears of regret and gratitude that the old lady had provided such a sanctuary dampened her lashes. Seeing them, Cathy offered to make tea, giving Helen a few moments alone.

Over a cup of tea and a 'wee strupack' that was considerably more than the snack the word suggested, Cathy told her about the shop, how it opened twice a week and had an informal policy that meant if anyone ran out they'd knock at the cottage door.

She listened but it all seemed very unreal to her. So much so that the task of sorting through her aunt's things and her tentative exploration of the island occupied her time almost exclusively. She was in a world of her own, a world of strangeness and delight, and it wasn't until she got back to the cottage one day to find James Frazer sitting waiting outside in the Land Rover that the realities of life on Cladach became clear.

'Hello, there.' His smile was warm. 'I expected to find Cathy here. Has she deserted you already?'

Experience as an interviewer suggested that his tone was just a bit too casual, but this was lost in the realisation that the shop was supposed to open that day.

'Oh, I'm terribly sorry.' She quickly unlocked the door. 'Cathy did tell me the opening times, but I thought...' She had never considered running the shop. Had she expected them all to do without supplies while she had a holiday? 'Have I missed a lot of people?'

'There have been a few grumbles.' James frowned, his pleasant features showing displeasure. 'Cathy should have given you time to settle in. It's very bad of her. I'll have a word.'

'Oh, no, please don't.' Helen's green eyes were troubled. 'It was my fault. I should have taken more notice of what she was telling me. Everything is clearly marked; I won't have any trouble with the prices.'

Their conversation was brought to a halt by the arrival of other islanders.

'*Tha la math ann. Ciamar a tha thu?*' she was greeted over and over again. It was the Gaelic equivalent of 'Hello. How are you?' and that at least she had learnt, perched on Aunt Fi's knee, many years ago.

'*Tha gu math. Ciamar a tha sibh fhein?*' She said she was well and asked after their own health in return. It exhausted her knowledge of Gaelic, except for the odd word here and there, but the island people seemed pleased by the courtesy.

Helen spent the rest of the afternoon fully occupied, filling orders and trying to understand the heavily accented English spoken by the older inhabitants.

I'll have to learn Gaelic, she decided absently, and it wasn't until her last customer had gone that she realised just what that implied. She made herself a pot of tea and took it into the parlour. Evening sunshine gave a mellow warmth to the room, the smell of peat and heather drifting in through the window. 'I'm hooked,' she admitted to herself. Whatever her reasons for needing Cladach so intensely at that particular time in her life, she owed it to Aunt Fi to enjoy more of her home than the proceeds from the sale.

'What haunts you, fair Helen?' The lazy drawl made her look sideways to find Rick Cameron's face very near to her own.

'I was planning my shopping list,' she attempted to deflate him, but didn't succeed.

'Liar.' His voice was soft and intimate. 'Tell me and lay your ghosts. Strangers have strong magic, and I come from a long line of noble warriors.'

Humour lightened her eyes. 'Story-tellers, maybe.'

'See? You're feeling better already.'

Helen chuckled, aware of the low, musical quality of his own laughter. Life, she mused, was stranger than fiction. Rick Cameron was there to prove it.

CHAPTER TWO

'TERRIFIC.' Rick Cameron viewed the rain running down the windows of the carriage and narrowed his eyes as lightning tore up the sky. 'I think we're going to be late arriving,' he commented drolly as they slowed to a shuddering halt for the third time. 'Have you booked a room at Mallaig, or were you counting on getting through to Skye?'

'Skye.' She sounded as depressed about the situation as she felt.

'Well, you're not going to make the ferry.'

Accepting that this was true, Helen accustomed herself to the chore of finding a room.

'I know a place.' Rick Cameron's offer received a surprised and then dubious look. 'There's going to be a race once we're off the train.'

'I suppose British Rail will have arranged something.'

'Fine. If you want to spend the night in a church hall on a camp bed, it's up to you.'

Helen doubted it would be that bad but accepted that the restriction on accommodation was likely to be a problem. The tourist trade was heavily dependent on American tourists visiting their roots, and that year, she knew from her contacts in the trade, the figures were up. The chances of being recognised if she became one of the temporary refugees argued on the side of accepting Cameron's offer, but she had her reservations.

'Are you sure there will be space?'

'Trust me.' He smiled at the hesitancy he saw in her eyes. 'Hey, if I made a habit of kidnapping beautiful women everyone would know about it.'

She had reason to question his assurance when they arrived at a country cottage miles away from Mallaig with no apparent neighbours.

'There's a housekeeper.' Rick Cameron opened the door of the hired Metro which had been conveniently waiting for him in the station car park. Rain rushed in and she heard him mutter under his breath as the deluge engulfed him. He went to the back of the car. Helen cursed herself for being so gullible and remained mutinously inside the vehicle.

'Helen . . . ?' He came back to the open door, viewing her disenchantment, water dripping from his hair. 'What's wrong?' His eyes ran over her, the hard glitter in them showing that he guessed her thoughts. 'I guess you need proof of my good intentions.'

The proof produced itself. A stout woman, dressed in a candlewick dressing-gown, peered out into the darkness. 'You're late, Rick. I'd almost given you up.' Helen's eyes flew to the woman in surprise.

'Sleeping in the car?' Rick openly mocked her, pulling back, leaving the boot open so that she could take out whatever she needed. His uncompromising back view told her that he had run out of chivalry.

'Away in with you. It's a terrible night. I'll put on the cocoa.'

The cocoa convinced her. Helen grabbed her handbag and emerged into a torrential downpour. In seconds her hair was plastered to her head, and retrieving her overnight case seemed a marathon effort. She staggered towards the warm lights of the cottage.

Peggy MacDonald eyed the young woman accompanying Rick Cameron and then gave him a reproving sniff, which made him smile. He took off his jacket, the dark T-shirt he wore showing the rain had got through.

'It's not the way you think, Peggy.' He put his hands up as if warding off a stream of words. 'Helen was stranded by the bad weather. She helped me keep a low profile on the train. I could hardly leave her to fend for herself.'

'I doubt you care much for the propriety of the thing.' Twinkling eyes showed a sense of humour. 'But if it's innocent help you're offering it will stay that way under this roof.'

'I think the young lady is rather determined on that score.' Rick turned to study Helen, who was peering at him from under a sheaf of wet hair.

'This isn't a hotel,' she pointed out coolly.

'Did I say it was?' Hands on hips, he returned the accusing gaze, his own warm with an appreciation that made Helen feel rather hollow inside. She felt hungry, and an awful suspicion grew that it wasn't for food. Her eyes lost their coldness and took on the feline quality that had attracted male viewers by the score to the TV programmes she had worked on. Then that sudden shift of mood had been caused by the memory of a beautiful place that had appealed to her senses or some cause that had touched her soul. Rick Cameron came into neither of these categories.

Two mugs of cocoa were put down on the table with slightly more emphasis than was necessary. Helen blinked and thanked the woman for her kindness, flushing faintly at the warning in the pale blue eyes holding hers for a second.

'Don't keep her up all night talking. The lassie's tired. I'm to my bed.' Peggy MacDonald retreated from the scene, leaving unspoken rules behind her.

'She makes me feel as if I'm ten and I've broken every rule in the book.' Rick grimaced ruefully. 'I've never dared tell her, but I hate this muck.' He got up and poured his cocoa into the sink. After foraging in the pantry for a few minutes he returned with a bottle of whisky.

'She knows you're a rascal and adores you for it.' Helen refused to be convinced by his boyish protestations. She wasn't quick enough to prevent the generous splash of the golden liquid that was supposed to improve her own beverage.

'So do you, apparently. But I don't know about adoration. I think, my lovely Helen, that, with a little more whisky warming your blood and the absence of our chaperon, you might loosen that strait-jacket you're in and have some fun.'

'Fun?' A fine eyebrow raised itself sceptically.

'Never come across the word?' Deliberately provocative, he sat on the table, close to where she was sitting. Crossing his arms, he returned the hostile glare with a flare of predatory excitement. 'I'm talking about letting your hair down, releasing the tension. You come on like one of these cold, hard career types, but your eyes are something else.'

'Could you show me my room?' She refused to rise to the bait, although her temper was beginning to simmer.

'Certainly,' he drawled, his gaze remaining on her cool features, an admiring glint recognising her forbearance. 'If you're looking to make a quick escape tomorrow morning, take the Metro. Leave it where we picked it up. There'll be no charge for the room.' He led the way out of the warm kitchen down a dimly lit passageway.

Helen Howard felt uncomfortable with herself for the umpteenth time in their short relationship. Now she felt rude, as if her reaction to his teasing had been way over the top. Was she a prude? Had Gary Chambers and Michael Burton made her into one of those cold, no-nonsense women who were totally out of their depth in male company?

'Thank you.' She accepted the key to the Metro as he paused in the doorway of the room she had been given.

'I think the storm's over. But if it comes back I'm just across the hallway. You can hide under my covers.'

Her chin lifted. He enjoyed tormenting her, she could see it in his eyes. 'I'm not frightened of storms,' she lied. 'I won't disturb you. Thank you for your help, Mr Cameron. You've been very kind.'

'Mmmm.' He didn't sound as if he was agreeing with her, his eyes dark now in the dim light, searching the fine planes of her face as if submitting them to memory. 'Goodnight, Helen. The offer stands; I'm a very light sleeper.'

'So am I,' she muttered under her breath, and she heard his low laughter as he disappeared into his own bedroom.

The next morning she was up at half-past six. The train journey and the subsequent events seemed strangely unreal and she intended to take up Rick Cameron's offer to use the Metro.

Fate didn't intend to let her off lightly. She was tip-toeing down the stairs when a huge, hairy hound bounded up to her and barked enthusiastically.

'Down, Jet!' Rick Cameron calmed the dog from his vantage-point at the top of the stairs.

Helen felt very foolish, realising he must have watched her trying to avoid detection.

'I give all my women breakfast.' Rick leant against the banister, just waiting for the fireworks.

'You're right, Mr Cameron, you have been very bored.' She spoke in a heated undertone. 'It seems making people uncomfortable has become a sport with you.'

'Some people make themselves uncomfortable, my dear,' he returned smoothly. The 'my dear' was borrowed from some Deep South melodrama and laughed at her outrage. 'What can I get you? Eggs and bacon, toast, or do you eat that organic junk? Grapefruit's my guess.' He continued to bait her as he came down the stairs, the hound Jet having the bad taste to leap at him and attempt to lick him.

'I'd just like to be on my way, if you don't mind.'

'But I do.' He approached her and she began to back down the stairs until she realised what she was doing, and stood her ground with growing agitation as he came threateningly close. Dressed in blue jeans, a navy jumper and a pale grey body warmer, he looked well equipped for the capricious Highland weather. 'I hate eating breakfast alone.' The smile in his eyes was positively indecent. For one mind-blowing second Helen almost believed they had spent the night together!

'You've kindly allowed me the use of your car.' She tried valiantly to stop the blush as his eyes wandered over her face as she spoke, examining her eyes, the small straight nose and her lips as if he were studying some artwork he intended to buy. 'I'm eager to be on my way.' Her lips quivered slightly as he watched the words form and then looked her straight in the eyes. Leaving nothing of his thoughts hidden, he did make her blush, and, laughing low in his throat, he passed her by.

'I've got the key to let you out. It's in the pocket of my jeans.' He slapped his thigh revealingly. 'I wouldn't dream of keeping you prisoner; you can get it if you like.'

'You disgusting...' Words failed her. Futile seconds of outrage later, she decided she was achieving nothing standing in the hallway, and followed him reluctantly to the kitchen.

Regarding him with loathing from the doorway, she saw the promised grapefruit residing in a breakfast bowl.

'I hate grapefruit.' She walked over to the table and sat down, regarding his activities with distrust.

'You can sweeten it up a bit with sugar,' he suggested innocently, bringing a huge, steaming pot of tea to the table.

'No, thank you. I'll just have tea.'

'You're going to fade away.' He regarded her figure this time with a practised air. 'You can't weigh more than——'

'I know what I weigh. I'm not dieting. Surprisingly enough——' she was cutting '—I've lost my appetite.'

'You're a hard woman to please.' He poured her tea and pushed the cup and saucer across to her.

'You could please me by letting me go.' Green eyes met hazel with purposeful intent.

'Where to? Wherever it is, you're behind schedule. I could——'

'No, thank you, Mr Cameron. I think I've had quite enough of your help.'

'And I think...' he rested his arms on the table, leaning forward slightly '...that you are more than you seem. Most highly efficient businesswomen would either cash in on meeting me or brush me off without turning a hair. All the signals I'm getting tell me you're not capable of doing either. So you're either a babe in arms pretending to be sophisticated, or you're very clever and are ninety-nine per cent of the way to having me fooled.'

She looked startled. Of course, it must seem odd. She had accepted his offer of accommodation because the alternative promised to expose her to unwelcome publicity. But, from his point of view, he must have thought that she was overwhelmed by his star status and undoubted good looks or that she was going to use the incident for some publicity purpose. Since she had refused to share his bed, she couldn't blame him for being suspicious. He was clearly as eager to protect his privacy as she was, which made his offer to share the cottage a bit odd. Why had he prolonged their acquaintance? Remembering the incident on the stairs, the question died as it formed on her lips. Whatever his motivation, she was convinced his answer would bring a rosy glow to her cheeks, and she was rather tired of playing court jester.

'I just wanted a room for the night.' She avoided looking at him, sipping her tea. 'I thought you meant a hotel, you know that.'

'Sure.' He didn't look convinced. 'You want to be careful. You could get yourself into a lot of trouble.'

Raising incredulous eyes to his face, she saw that he was serious, although a glimmer of amusement appeared at her expression. 'I mean it. Some guys wouldn't be content to listen to you twist and turn all night—they'd want to cure your restlessness.'

'Supposing you could.' She had her back against the wall and was willing to fight.

'Oh, I could.' He smiled at her with such sexual promise that her heart jolted, her skin prickling with intense awareness.

Rick Cameron watched Helen's eyes dilate with a sharpness of anticipation that was totally unjustified by any promise of fulfilment. It had been quite a while since a woman had excited him so much; in fact, he couldn't remember when one had. It went back to adolescence and that sweet fascination with sex that exaggerated any encounter with an attractive female. It was the pull she exerted on him that made him suspicious. Not many people could get to him, and the fact that she could made him wary but intrigued.

'I've had my tea.' Helen was determined to be put off no longer. This man made her feel unsafe with a look. Michael Burton seemed small beer in comparison. 'I want to go now, please.'

'We'll go together. That way, I won't have a host of reporters at my heels.'

Helen felt her heart sink to her boots. Would she ever be free of the man? Last night he had offered her the use of the car. Without such a promise of freedom she doubted she would have endured the night in the cottage. It had been a false promise, of course; he had known all along she couldn't get out without a key.

'For someone so keen to avoid the Press,' she commented acidly, 'you seem intent on providing me with a good story.'

His gaze sharpened, but the mockery was still apparent. 'The papers will print anything, but I think the libel laws would make mincemeat of a story suggesting I coerced you in any way. You came with me of your own free will. I gave you shelter for the night, a lift into Mallaig. No, I think you might come out of the whole thing looking a little bit ungrateful.'

'I'll resist the temptation to send you a thank-you letter.' She mutinously returned his regard. 'How long do you think you'll be?'

'Not long.' He stood up, winking at her suspicious expression. 'Something you'll have to learn is patience, especially on the islands. Time doesn't have quite the same meaning there as in London.'

She knew that. But the knowledge that he knew it too worried her. There was something intense about her relationship with Rick Cameron. She felt too many emotions in his presence, feelings that were strange and new, but no less powerful for that. It didn't seem credible that this infuriating man was going to make a quick exit from her life, even when she felt it was imperative that he should do so.

The morning was a mixture of sun and cloud but it didn't look like rain, Helen noticed absently as she at last gained her freedom and waited with a noticeable lack of patience while Rick Cameron put his holdall into the boot.

Opening the door for her, he made a mock bow at her disdainful expression. She dragged the seatbelt across her body as he closed the door with a smart click, shifting as far away from the driver's seat as possible when he joined her in the car.

'I'll give you a tip about men.' He couldn't resist the temptation to rile her. 'They prefer a sweet-tempered woman in the morning.'

Helen gave him a glacial stare and then deliberately turned her head to take in the scenery, determined not to speak a word until they reached Mallaig and she could continue her journey. As it was, he switched on the radio, and the atmosphere in the car became decidedly more relaxed. From that point on Rick Cameron seemed to dismiss her from his mind. He drove with skill, the few miles to Mallaig eaten up in less than twenty minutes, making Helen aware of how careful he had been the night before. It had been an hour before they had reached the Highland cottage.

Pulling up near the harbour, Rick Cameron unloaded her luggage, looking down at the young woman as she checked everything was there. She, too, wore jeans, and a bright red blouson-style jacket that was cheerful and warm.

'Got everything?' He smiled down at her, his eyes telling her that he thought her refusal to let him help any further rather ridiculous.

'Yes.' She swung her own holdall over her shoulder and picked up the two large suitcases. The last thing she wanted was for him to find out where she was going.

'Until the next time, Helen.' He bent and brushed her lips with his, moving back as her mouth formed on a torrent of protest.

Dropping her cases, she gazed in impotent protest at his retreating back. How stupid of her to immobilise herself in such a manner, giving him an opportunity to... What? A saner voice cooled her chagrin. He was teasing her because he thought her starchy, and disapproval of his own easy sexuality was over the top. With a wan smile at her own reaction to the man she realised more than ever that she needed a break. Cladach was her haven; this brief sojourn with the 'on the run' film star had brought back unwelcome complications into her life. Her new island home was small enough to get to know the entire population and the security of that made her reflect on her own bid for escape. Was she really that frightened of some male taking over her life? The storm, the feeling of being temporarily homeless and the need to depend on Rick Cameron for safety and shelter had left her feeling decidedly unsettled. For a moment her mind flitted to her mother and the dark days after John Howard, her father, had died. She had found Moira Howard's grief and aching loneliness frightening. She had been only thirteen at the time, and for one parent to die and the other to be virtually rubbed out as a recognisable personality had scared her. To love that deeply... it was such a risk!

Crossing the water to Skye made her breathe a sigh of relief. She felt as if she had finally escaped Rick Cameron's clutches. That kind of man was too much of a danger. She wasn't blind to or untouched by male potency. He had stirred reluctant emotions within her, making her want to match her wits against his, duel with that tense sexual awareness that... Her teeth ground against each other.

'Carry on like that, my girl,' she muttered, 'and you'll be turning back.' Grinning at her own humour, she cast her mind over her transport difficulties. She'd need to get a taxi to Uig Bay. The ferry left from the north-west of Skye, and the bus route was not exactly frequent.

Her return to the island took up most of the day. Murdo Buchanan was willing to take her across the sound, but not until he'd taken care of some business. She discovered the islanders hadn't been convinced she'd return, but the hospitality when she got there was gratifying. Cathy Ferguson came down to the bay to meet the boat in a battered-looking Ford. She helped Helen with her cases and then drove her the short distance to the cottage. Over a late tea Cathy brought her up to date with the happenings in the shop.

'It's a good thing you've come back.' Cathy's dark head bobbed over her teacup as if she was disguising her expression. 'I'll be leaving for Aberdeen. I'm off to the big city.' She looked up, a self-deprecating smile pulling at the corners of her mouth. 'So I won't be able to help in the shop.'

'Do you want to leave?' Helen didn't like to think her arrival was driving the girl out.

'Och, it's nothing to do with you.' Cathy smiled, but managed to look wistful at the same time. 'I've been meaning to go for a few years now, but I get nothing from my man but promises. So...' She shrugged and said no more on the subject.

'You're using dynamite?' Helen chuckled.

'Maybe.' An answering gleam of humour lit the other woman's eyes. 'Now, what haven't I told you? Did the solicitor explain about the croft?' She sighed when she saw Helen's blank expression. 'You'd better speak to James about it. There's no rush. Basically, the cottage is yours but the croft is still part of the estate. You're a tenant with a bundle of rights that no one has quite fathomed yet, but if you want to you can continue to farm it.'

Island life and its supposed simplicity seemed to Helen to be getting more complicated by the minute. The conversation turned to the local inhabitants after the business side had been dealt with. Cathy's father, Helen discovered, managed the whisky distillery, which employed several of the islanders, for the Frazers. She also had a brother, who was equally keen to leave Cladach. James Frazer, she revealed, was unmarried, and his sister had kept the family name by persuading Andy McFee, her husband, to change his. Helen remarked on the unusual nature of the arrangement, but Cathy merely shrugged, not willing to gossip about her friends, although her manner indicated that there was a lot left unsaid.

'Oh...' Cathy was a little too casual, turning at the door before she left for her own home '... James asked me to pass on his invitation to Castealcreag. I've left the number by the phone, if you want to have a word with him; otherwise they'll expect you tomorrow for tea.'

'Thank you.' Helen didn't know what to make of Cathy's tone but she knew something wasn't right. 'I'm grateful for all the help you've given me.'

Cathy nodded. 'I won't be a stranger. If you're in trouble just shout.'

After she'd gone Helen looked out at the clouds gathering and decided to call it a day. She hadn't slept much the night before, and the thought of the nice comfortable bed was irresistible.

Helen woke up the next morning to the unfamiliar sound of exuberant gulls. Light from the small windows slashed across the lemon candlewick, and as she propped herself up on her elbows the cotton sheet almost crackled. For a few seconds Helen was lost. The old-fashioned dressing-table and the small bedside table with its lamp and home-made shade were totally alien.

Memory rushed back, and she relaxed against the plump pillows, breathing in the faint aroma of violets that scented the sheets.

'Samhrad Taigh,' she said softly, feeling she was trying to capture a dream that might fade with the oncoming of consciousness.

Butterflies played havoc with her stomach and she experienced a sense of nervous anticipation not felt since childhood. Her travel clock showed it was just past seven, and she threw back the covers and went to the window. Opening the flowered curtains, she saw Jessie, the cow, in the field, contentedly munching grass. The sky was unrelentingly blue, not a cloud anywhere. Jessie's tail

swished busily as she dislodged flies, and a nearby bee
buzzed busily around a clump of thistles.

'It's doing its best to impress you, Helen.' She tried
to curb the burst of happiness that threatened to engulf
her. 'Everywhere looks nice when the sun shines.'

Fighting the intoxicating effect her first day back on
the island was having on her, Helen steadfastedly prepared breakfast. She supposed she should go through
the check-list Cathy had prepared for her, but then her
mind swung on to the subject of the weather. It could
change without warning. She would feel cheated if she
spent all morning in the shop and then had a wet
afternoon to spend twiddling her thumbs.

Unable to be sensible any longer, she dressed in jeans
and a brightly coloured jumper, packed a picnic and was
on her way. Helen decided to follow the coastline northwards from Cladach Bagh. The island only covered forty
square miles, and a good proportion of that, she knew,
was peat bog and loch. It would be easier to retrace her
steps if she followed the coastal path; she didn't want
to make a nuisance of herself by getting lost. It was a
busy island, and they hadn't time to look for foolhardy
tourists. Yet the desire to meet Cladach and see it through
eyes that were new, not coloured by love or, as in Cathy's
case, frustration, was important to her.

Retracing the journey she had made previously by car,
she found herself noticing much more detail. Although
the sea was visible from Samhrad Taigh, it was over a
mile to the jetty. It was easy to guess why there was no
sign of habitation nearer to Cladach Bagh. Heather and
bracken dominated with bushes of wild, prickly gorse.
It was rocky and hostile, and it would have been a brave
man who tried to reclaim the land for the plough.

Helen was out of breath by the time she reached the
cliff path. She stopped to look out to sea, her eyes seeking
and finding the outline of Barra. Although Britain was
an island, Helen had never been conscious of it as such.

On Cladach it would be impossible to forget. The sea
was their bounty and their curse. It fed them and kept
them isolated, so that the neighbouring island of Barra
might as well have been as far away as the moon when
a storm howled in from the Atlantic over Cladach Sound.
Helen had heard the far-flung St Kilda referred to as 'the
island on the edge of the world', but for her Cladach
was that. She wanted to be far away from her old life,
and that morning, as she'd woken in the sun-splashed
bedroom, London had seemed a million miles away.

The wind was stronger near the cliff edge and it rushed
past Helen's ears, enclosing her, making her a prisoner
of its sea-song. The hot blood reddening her cheeks
cooled, and reluctantly she tore her gaze from the expanse of blue and began to follow the coastal path. She
decided to use her watch as a gauge of distance, reck-
oning that an hour's walking would represent four miles
if the terrain wasn't too difficult. In that calculation she
was bedevilled. The path was tortuous. When an hour
was up she was unable to make a guess at her progress
other than to say it was slow. She was about to give up
when the path widened, and she looked down on to a
rocky bay.

The east coast of the island did not have the white
sand that formed an attractive feature of the west. It
provided safe harbourage, not exposed to the open
Atlantic. Sea pink and golden rod helped to decorate the
bare habitat, and a profusion of birds wheeled and dived
over the thin ribbon of sand and battery of rocks. The
remains of a boat, tipped at a crazy angle, attracted
Helen's attention. The sea had receded with the tide.
She made for the boat, planning to find a dry rock near
by as a picnic spot.

It was more difficult to get to than she had thought.
Her shoes were soaked as she slipped in and out of the
shallow pools left by the sea. As she got closer she could
see the old timber flaking in the sun. Its stern was sub-

merged in the depths of a rocky pool, seaweed and ane-
mones visible, the sunlight just penetrating deep enough
to reveal the surprised crab scuttling away from the small
pebbles Helen had dislodged.

Gazing out to sea, Helen watched what looked like a
clumsy gull patter along the surface of the water to get
into the air. It wasn't a gull, she decided; maybe it was
a fulmar, the bird whose oil had kept the cruisies lit on
dark winter nights.

Finding her rock, she winced a little at the hardness
of the surface but commenced with the ritual of laying
out the small cloth she had brought and spreading out
the various items making up her lunch.

A noise just in front of her made her look up sharply
to meet a puffin eyeing her with curiosity from a neighbouring rock. Helen laughed, her eyes shining.

'Do you want to share my picnic?' She adopted a
solemn tone. The bird put its head to the side as if considering the offer. Its beak, as always, attracted attention with the basal blue-grey separated by a yellow
ridge from the red tip. It wasn't very interested in the
bread she threw but kept her company while she ate.

Why had Aunt Fi never said 'Come to Cladach. You
can picnic with puffins'? Perhaps she had, but Moira
Howard had been against the place and children were
very susceptible to their parents' influence. Besides the
pressure brought by Helen's grandmother, Moira
Howard's idea of a holiday was a visit to Paris or Rome.
Helen recalled her mother's restlessness when they had
visited the country or the seaside. 'Whatever do they
find to do here?' had been her verdict on such places,
and Helen's lips tilted into an affectionate smile. Cladach
would not suit her mother one bit.

Returning to her cottage several hours later, she found
that she was just in time to open the shop. While she
served her customers her mind went over the possibilities in her wardrobe for tea at Castealcreag. The name

conjured up something from another age. When she had questioned Cathy on the subject she had just smiled and told her to wait and see.

She decided to wear a tan suede jacket and matching skirt. The jacket was cropped, double-breasted with suede-covered buttons. The skirt moulded her hips and flared out mid-thigh to rest just below her knee. A silky gold top and matching earrings and watch enhanced the rich golden colour of her hair. The effect had a strange blend of ease and formality that marked her own particular style. Many of her fan letters had begged to know where she shopped, but Helen's taste was so varied and largely instinctive that her reticence on the subject had sometimes been attributed to coyness.

The toot on the horn of the Land Rover made Helen hurriedly collect her handbag. As she locked the door of the shop the sound of a helicopter in the distance made her search the skies.

'It's away to the west,' Andy Frazer informed her, a smile lighting up his face.

Helen's curiosity satisfied itself with the possibilities of an air search or perhaps a delivery from the mainland and she was distracted by the need to slide herself into the waiting vehicle.

The journey to Castealcreag took a little under half an hour, and Helen was sure that she had felt every bump on the extremely uneven road surface. However, her aches and pains were forgotten when she saw Castealcreag for the first time.

'It's a castle,' she breathed in childlike wonder, and Andy grinned.

'I'm a prince—did you not guess? My wife will be only too happy to bore you with the details. She's very keen on tradition.'

Castealcreag looked over the long, sweeping bay out to the Atlantic. White shell sand gleamed under the stroke of the capricious sun, and the machair formed a

belt of green that gave the western coast a fertility denied
the east. The castle was rooted in the rock. It had a square
keep tower, and inside the courtyard Andy pointed out
the chapel, now used by the whole island, and the hall,
which was put into service for the ceilidhs that were held
monthly. It had been modernised, of course, with an eye
to preserving tradition.

Helen was taken to a drawing-room overlooking the
bay and served tea by the housekeeper, an elderly
woman, introduced as Mary MacInnes.

The furniture was Regency and set an elegant tone,
the predominant colour a subdued green, lightened here
and there by subtle touches of gold tooled into the
woodwork of the couches and repeated in a pencil-thin
stripe on their silk upholstery. Sheepskin rugs stretched
in front of a magnificent fireplace, bringing an island
touch to a room that would otherwise not be out of place
anywhere where there was wealth coupled with good
taste. Helen smiled at her own thoughts. What had she
expected? Walls covered with stags' heads and tartan
carpets?

Sarah Frazer joined them. She was similar in colouring
to her brother James and was heavily pregnant. Helen
couldn't help wondering why Sarah wasn't on the
mainland. Surely it was a risk to both mother and child
being so far away from a hospital?

'Are you really planning to live in Fiona's cottage?'
Sarah Frazer didn't waste time on curiosity. 'It's a hard
life if you're not born to it. I think you should think
the matter over very carefully.'

Helen was taken aback, but her journalistic training
kept her from showing it.

'Take your time, lassie,' Andy intervened. 'For a
Hebridean, Sally's always trying to get things sorted out.
She doesn't like things being left in the air.'

Sarah Frazer leapt on his words, her eyes over-bright.
'I'm sure I do nothing of the sort. People don't realise

how delicately balanced island life is. If we want to stay a viable community——'

'On your soap box again, Sally.' James Frazer's entrance had a miraculously calming effect on his sister. She subsided and gave a girlish laugh.

'Poor Helen.' Her colour remained high. 'I'm afraid the problems of depopulation are a pet subject with me. James has tried so hard to stop the rot.' She gave him an affectionate smile.

'I think we should let Helen settle in before we get her on to that one.' James Frazer's easy manner defused any tension that existed, so much so that Helen wondered if she had imagined it.

She didn't imagine Andy's muttered, 'Always the diplomat,' and surmised that island life, as all things, held its own tensions and intrigues.

Helen found herself becoming fascinated by the tapestry of life on Cladach. It was different from anything she had ever known. During tea she discovered that Andy's family ran Cladach's fishing industry. He jokingly referred to it as the 'coracle fleet'. It comprised of three fishing boats and its main activity was in the summer months, following the run of the herring and trapping lobsters. Sarah found her subject in the decline of the fishing industry and the damage done by outsiders fishing the Hebridean waters. She was an independence movement all on her own, her affinity to Cladach and its history verging on the obsessional. Her child would have the family name; perhaps she hoped it would eventually become laird if it was a boy. If James didn't marry—he must be already nearing forty, Helen surmised—then Sarah's son would inherit. It came as something of a surprise to find there was a younger brother.

Helen remarked on a photograph framed on the wall when a pause developed in the conversation. It had considerable charm and had been catching her eye for some time. Three children played in a boat, a small boy standing on the prow, his arms spread wide, claiming the world before him.

'Young Frazer and his crew.' James grinned but there was a wistful note to his voice.

'He always was an exhibitionist.' Sarah dismissed the photograph, despite the fact that the chubby-cheeked toddler tugging at the little boy's shirt must have been her. At the back of the boat sat an older boy—James, she recognised easily. He was laughing and pointing at something as if to distract the younger children's attention from their game of 'king of the castle'.

'My brother doesn't live on the island.' James answered the question that hung on the air. 'I'm afraid he matched my father for stubbornness and temper. The place wasn't big enough for the both of them.'

The cowboy impersonation proved James something of a mimic. She remembered the accuracy of pitch when he had imitated her aunt imparting a secret. Helen laughed and so did Andy. But Sarah didn't laugh. She got up, the heat back in her cheeks.

'He's nothing like Father.' She put her hand at her back and walked heavily to the door. 'The island bored him. He was just looking for an excuse. If young Frazer had his head…' she waved contemptuously at the picture '…Cladach would be knee-deep in hamburgers and fruit machines.'

A noise at the door and Mrs MacInnes's voice clearly welcoming made Sarah stand back. Helen was sure her heart missed a beat as a nightmare unfolded itself in front of her very eyes. Rick Cameron came into the room, his eyes flicking over the inhabitants and then locking with her own.

'I don't know what your game is, sweetheart, but I, for one, am uncomfortable with an unemployed TV journalist on my doorstep!'

CHAPTER THREE

THE frozen tableau that followed Rick Cameron's words melted into a battery of questions.

'Explain yourself, Rick. Helen is our guest. Your manner is offensive.' James Frazer's disapproval reprimanded the outburst.

'We'll have Cladach overrun with journalists if they find out he's here,' Sarah Frazer added with some satisfaction.

'Helen is Fiona MacSween's great-niece. She inherited Samhrad Taigh.' Andy Frazer emphasised, 'She's to run the shop.'

'Oh, really?' Rick Cameron sneered. 'Look at her. She's hardly the shopkeeper type. There's been some sort of bust-up at Metro TV. She resigned in a huff. Now she's got the Press hungry for a story. If she's down on her luck she doesn't have to look far to make some money, does she?'

Helen rose to her feet, facing the blazing accusation in Rick Cameron's eyes. 'What are you doing here? I have no intention of contacting the Press whatsoever. I have never been involved in that kind of journalism and never will be.' Her indignation was plain to see. 'I certainly don't need the sort of publicity you would bring me, Mr Cameron. Your presence here is as abhorrent to me as mine seems to be to you!'

'Fine words.' He glowered at her. 'This happens to be my home. A fact I have managed to keep out of the news quite successfully. I need you like a hole in the head.'

'Likewise,' she snapped and then, conscious of the other occupants of the room, she felt a rush of shame. 'I'm terribly sorry. Perhaps I'd better leave...'

'Certainly not.' James Frazer wouldn't hear of it. 'Rick, if you can't be civil you can leave the room. I won't have guests accused in such a manner, especially when they are kin of such as Fiona MacSween.'

Taking a deep breath, Rick Cameron controlled his temper with difficulty. Pushing a hand through his hair, he glanced over at James Frazer.

'Maybe it is some grotesque coincidence. Does your show get transmitted here?' His eyes once again interrogated her.

'I've no idea. It's a travel programme called *Chase the Sun*,' she revealed grudgingly, her resentment plain to see. 'It won't be networked until the spring, anyway.'

'I've never seen it.' Sarah Frazer appeared to enjoy the situation. 'I apologise for my brother, Helen; he's unbearably ill-mannered.'

Brother! Helen's eyes flew to the photograph. Why hadn't she seen the resemblance? Rick Cameron was the missing Frazer!

'Why aren't you on the mainland?' The errant film star turned his attention to his sister, irritation clearly expressed. 'One twinge and I'll personally put you in that helicopter——'

'Rick!' James Frazer's exasperation was almost humorous.

'I'm going. I need a shower and a drink.' He cast Helen a dark, devilish look before opening the door. 'We'll talk later. Maybe over breakfast. You can cook this time.'

The man was a monster! A glassy smile rebuffed the onslaught of eyes. 'I—er—it isn't the way it sounds,' she began, her cheeks glowing.

Cladach had suddenly become dangerous and unsafe. Rick Cameron, by some devilment of fate, was the laird's brother, with every intention, it seemed, of staying on

the island. Why he was there was still a mystery, but it
didn't change the facts. He had insulted her, accused her
of the worst journalistic instincts, but dislike was hardly
a defence against such a forceful character. Despite his
accusations and anger, there had been something else in
his eyes that made her want to run.

Conversation after her embarrassed explanation of
Rick's blatant innuendo became superficial and a little
forced. Helen was glad to climb back into the Land Rover
and leave the oppressive confines of Castealcreag for the
relative tranquillity of Samhrad Taigh.

'You mustn't mind Rick.' Andy Frazer leant against
the wheel of the Land Rover as she found her key to the
cottage. 'James is still weak from the accident, and
Sarah's being so stubborn about staying here to have the
baby troubles him. It troubles me.' He tried a grin but
the anxiety was there. 'He left here when he was sixteen
because of the way it was with his father; he doesn't
want to be exiled again. Cladach protects its own, Helen;
it will protect you if you let it.'

Catching Andy Frazer's eyes, she became aware of
the underlying threat. Should she betray Rick Cameron
to the Press she would get the same treatment handed
out to Clara MacSween. Cladach had two faces: it could
give shelter or exile. She nodded wordlessly. Time would
convince them of her sincerity; they didn't know her well
enough to accept her word.

Cathy Ferguson entered the shop the next day to find
Helen, hair tied back, examining the dusty boxes that
ranged high up on the walls and contained various unsold
items dating back years.

'Good lord.' She sneezed as a cloud of dust came up
from a box of children's socks. 'I don't think Aunt Fi
ever threw anything out,' she commented humorously.

'I did suggest it once.' Cathy grinned. 'How did your visit to the castle go? I hear that Roderick has honoured us with his presence. Did you see him?'

'Yes.' She couldn't keep the grim note out of her voice. 'If by Roderick you mean Rick Cameron. We met on the train to Mallaig. He's discovered I used to work for Metro TV so he accused me of having a hotline to Fleet Street.' She decided it was better to come clean and then was struck dumb by that idea that he must have gone through her things for some ID. She hadn't told him her second name.

Cathy's grin widened. 'He made a good impression, then. There used to be fireworks when old Frazer was alive. Roderick should have been laird. Och, I'm not being disloyal.' She interpreted Helen's surprised look. 'This place is in his blood. He would have brought it into the twentieth century. James just keeps things ticking over, and Sally... well, she'd have us all living in a museum.'

Helen privately thought Rick or Roderick was the rudest man she had ever met but, acknowledging Cathy's affection for the man, she kept her peace.

'I suppose he took Cameron as a stage name,' she reflected, unable to quench a spark of curiosity.

'Old Frazer refused to have anything to do with his acting career. Rick's full title is Roderick Cameron McKinnon Frazer. I suppose Rick Cameron is less of a mouthful, but the main reason he took the name was to divorce himself from any connection with the Frazers.' Cathy watched Helen tug down another box, a smile playing around her mouth. 'If you worked for the TV you should have a lot in common.'

Helen's snort of derision showed exactly what she thought of that, and her green eyes were faintly offended when she discovered Cathy's mirth as she came back down the small stepladder with the cardboard box.

'Unlike old Frazer, Rick does know how to apologise. I'm sure he'll realise his mistake.' Cathy's kindness soothed her somewhat.

Imagining Rick Cameron apologising was beyond her. She remembered the evening at the cottage near Mallaig. He could lure her into thinking she had misjudged him and then fling her straight back into battle again.

'Do you want some help?' Cathy eyed the boxes still stacked up to the ceiling.

'Thanks,' Helen accepted gratefully. 'But first, tea,' she suggested to the others girl's nod of agreement.

'I was thinking of putting up a list, asking for ideas for new lines for the shop,' she consulted the islander, putting the crockery on one of the small tables in the cottage's lounge.

'Good idea. You'll have to watch your overheads, though. The islanders aren't totally dependent on the shop. At this time of year regular trips to Skye or Oban are usual. We get a certain amount of tourists...' She was surprised by Helen's sudden pallor. 'Good gracious, you're not hiding away too, are you?'

'The Press can be a nuisance.' She played down her own notoriety. 'Rick's and my both being here would raise a few eyebrows.'

'I see.'

Helen received the impression that her new friend was amused by the bizarre complication to island life. They worked the rest of the morning clearing the backlog of ancient stock from the shelves. She discovered that the Frazer interests went further than farming. Apart from their abundance of sheep, they also distilled malt whisky, under the Castealcreag label. Most of it went to America, Cathy Ferguson informed her. The demand for bottled malt had increased by fifty per cent in the last five years, and apparently Rick Cameron's contacts had created an outlet for the company when small distilleries were being gobbled up by mighty conglomerates.

'Rick wanted to develop a hotel here. The other islands have made use of their lochs and scenery to give the population an income. Old Frazer wouldn't hear of it. James was willing to listen, but Sally put her foot down. Rick exploded into one of his tempers—he's not the world's best diplomat—and the idea was shelved. I think James tried to patch things up. He visited Rick in Los Angeles, but the crash...' She broke off, looking pained. 'Well, everything is in limbo again.'

Helen remained busy in the shop all afternoon. When she finally closed the door she decided to have a bath and go for a walk. The more she learned about the Frazers, the more likely it seemed that Rick Cameron was protecting some weighty skeletons. It must be a strange duality to live with, one half of him a media god of the new age, the other a younger son with ambitions to the throne of Cladach. James Frazer's affable leadership lacked something. Whatever old Frazer's strengths had been they had been handed down to the two younger members of the family.

She followed the path down to the bay with the shipwrecked boat. The photograph came back to mind and she realised that it must have been taken there. The tides and anger of the sea had made it settle deeper into its own small ocean. It was nearly covered now, the tide lapping at the narrow strip of the beach.

Sitting on a pile of rocks at the far end of the bay, she watched the breakers crash into a white froth on the rock shelf, fifteen metres away from where she was sitting. The waves looked like stretched glass, rearing up, almost solid, and then splintering into a million pieces.

Unaware of being watched, she wasn't conscious of the enchanting picture she made, her profile clear as she looked out into the compulsive obsession of the high tide, her honey-coloured hair swept over her shoulders, the collar of her short denim jacket turned up, the golden skin of her arms and throat glowing with health. Looped golden earrings gave her a vague gypsyish air. Jeans showed the length of her slim thighs. White canvas shoes protected her feet from the rocks, but otherwise she had that slick fashion sense that her observer was all too familiar with.

Rick Cameron had called his PR man after he had dropped Helen off at Mallaig harbour. He remembered the conversation well.

'Hi, Mel. Can you get me some background on someone?' He had listened for a moment to the squeaks of outrage about his desertion of the film set. 'I need some time and that's not up for discussion. All right. The lady in question is called Helen Howard... What do you mean, "*the* Helen Howard"? I've never heard of her. I'll give you the address.' He hadn't got much further.

'Helen Howard, my dear boy, has just pulled out of a contract race for a consumer programme in what sound like quite tacky circumstances. Something happened between her and Michael Burton, the producer. She's one of those pure, shining types that the English get hung up on. This latest episode has the Press salivating. She's more than a TV journalist, though; the TV ratings for her programmes have more to do with the young lady's personal charisma than anything she actually says. What's your interest?'

He had hung up. Hell, why had she stayed next to him on the train? They had doubled up their publicity value and chance of being seen just sharing the same carriage. No one was going to believe they weren't lovers, travelling together, spending the night in the cottage and now Cladach. Giving her a quick once over, he found he didn't mind that particularly; it just didn't fit in with his plans to have a slushy romantic hideaway story emanating from Cladach.

'Trying to get drowned?' he queried, letting his presence be known and watching the shocked flash of her eyes with satisfaction.

'What?'

'The tide. It's cut off the path.' He waved his hand negligently towards the other end of the bay.

'Oh.' Standing up, she was momentarily distressed. 'Is there another way up?'

'Naturally,' he returned, his mockery unsheathed. 'Otherwise I wouldn't be here. It's a hard climb, though.' His eyes flicked her canvas shoes. 'This isn't one of your civilised English holiday towns. If you're going to live here you'll have to learn to dress sensibly.'

Her eyes glowed with inner fire. 'I'm surprised you didn't leave me to drown. You could stop worrying about my being a Fleet Street mole then.'

'It's hard to keep death discreet.' His teeth flashed into a smile. 'I suppose I owe you an apology. If you're on the level, we're both in the same predicament.'

Regarding him steadily, Helen felt a distinct disinclination to believe him. He might have a hot temper but he wasn't stupid, and she suspected him of having ulterior motives for this sudden olive branch. After all, if his insufferable attitude had made her leave Cladach, the chances of her revealing his whereabouts were much greater.

'On the train you had a sense of humour,' he reminded her, going past her to leap agilely on one of the bigger rocks and open his arms to the sea. 'Roin Bagh. Seal Bay. Old Fiona wanted you here, did you know that? She said you belonged here...something to do with your soul. Do you still have a soul, Helen?' Cynical amusement was written all over him.

'Have you?' Helen muttered under her breath, to find laughing eyes fixed on her as he turned to view her, the sea in its roaring strength behind him. He must be used to finding good camera shots, she decided acidly, his feet resting firmly on the rock, peacock-blue T-shirt moulded lovingly across his chest, contrasting with the dark unruly hair and bringing out the blue lights in his hazel eyes.

'So...' He moved when the waves crashed a little too close for comfort, his hair curling with the sea-spray. Coming to stand within a pace of her, the interrogation began again. 'What brings a pretty girl like you to Cladach? The social life is an acquired taste. You'll spend a long time searching for a smart restaurant. Are the papers right? Are you running away from something?'

Her face clouded, the pleasure she had found in the beauty of the hidden bay drowned in unpleasant memories. 'Aren't we all?' she returned coolly, reflecting that he had his own share of secrets.

'It's painful, then,' he deduced with a similar lack of tact he'd shown on the train journey. 'Over? Or still a chance of reconciliation?'

The look she bestowed on him told of great irritation and would have quelled a lesser mortal.

'I've covered my tracks well, except for that débâcle on the train. Have you?' He lost interest in her for a moment, watching a cormorant drop like a stone into the sea. 'I don't want some guy with an eye to the main chance following you here.'

'I see.' Suddenly his interest became apparent. He wasn't bothered about any ties she might have; he just wanted to make sure he wasn't discovered. 'You needn't worry about that. No one will follow me here.'

'Must have ice in his veins.' The lazy charm was back, and she guessed it was second nature with him to flatter the opposite sex.

'I didn't say it was anything to do with a man—you did.'

'Something else?' he reflected as if they were playing a party game. 'No, it's a man. The way you look, it's got to be.'

Getting rather sick of the conversation, she gestured upwards. 'Shall we go?'

'This Michael Burton.' He walked around her as if she were some prize animal awaiting his inspection. 'Were you having an affair, or did he want your delectable body in exchange for anchoring that consumer programme?'

Goaded, she clenched her fists by her sides, restraining a host of new and very violent emotions. 'My,' she was vitriolic, 'we have been doing our homework. Have you had me investigated as well as going through my luggage?'

'I like to know who and what I'm dealing with.' Water foamed inches away from his feet. He barely noticed it.

Helen searched the cliff, panicked. The sound of the waves had become threatening, fast channels of water filling in the space between the rocks.

'Tell me or we'll both get very wet.'

A wave washed around his legs and Helen moved back. There seemed nowhere to go to. 'You're mad!' She couldn't believe he was serious.

A menacing smile touched his mouth. Another wave covered him to the knee, soaking the material of his jeans and bathing Helen's feet, creaming over her ankles. Another wave began to build behind them.

'Rick!'

Responding to her panic, he grasped her wrist, pulling her behind him in what seemed a dash into the path of the oncoming waves. It would never have occurred to Helen to go round the promontory and she found herself in shallow water, being led to a pebbled beach. A recognisable path led up the cliff.

'Of all the stupid, irresponsible things to do,' she accused him, her eyes viridescent, dragging her arm from his hold. Without thought of the consequences she aimed a slap at his mocking, amused face. It connected, and she had the satisfaction of seeing his head swing sideways. It didn't last long.

Grabbing hold of her wrist, he lost his grasp as she tugged desperately in the opposite direction. Racing across the sand, she felt him behind her as a physical weight despite the deadening of sound by the sand and the crash of the sea. A flying rugby tackle floored her. Twisting her head around to avoid getting sand in her mouth, she panted to drive some air back into her lungs.

'Touch me and I'll bite you,' she threatened, rage coursing through her blood.

'I think I might like that.' He pulled her round, his chest heaving, desire flaring in his eyes at the sight of her beneath him. The jacket had slipped free of its studs to show a white broderie anglaise sun-top, dragged down by the pressure of his body to show the golden curve of her breast.

'If Burton's had you he won't give up easily.'

Closing her eyes to shut him out, she almost screamed at the sheer dogged determination of the man. She had to get out of this situation quickly. Rick Cameron's hard weight against her was making her think of anything but their argument.

'It wasn't like that,' she denied, her eyes open, the colour a deep emerald-green.

'He wanted you to sleep with him to secure the contract.' Rick Cameron found himself relieved by the news; the peak of her nipple probing the edge of her sun-top wasn't doing much for his better instincts to let her up.

'Yes.' She licked lips that felt unaccountably dry.

'Poor baby.' His voice was like warm syrup sweetening her senses. 'Perhaps Fiona was right—maybe you do belong here.' Stroking her hair back from her forehead, he wondered how long it was going to take for her to recover her battling spirit. 'Mouth dry?' He caught sight of the pink tip of her tongue and resigned himself to following the demands of his masculine nature. Whatever was knocking her off balance he was selfish enough to exploit.

The touch of his lips seemed to come from a long way off. Rick's hand stroked her throat, grains of sand trickling down into the hollow at its base. His firm mouth nuzzled at her lips, easing them apart, the warm silk of his tongue pushing against her teeth.

There was nothing retributive about the way he kissed her. He was genuinely absorbed in her female beauty. At the back of her mind Helen had always suspected that what she aroused in men was purely illusory, a trick of the camera that had nothing to do with her at all.

The shock of his hand against her breast made her open her mouth to protest. A warm flood-tide of sweet passion surged through her veins, making the clutch of her hand on his arm barely condemnatory. His mouth moved over hers with increasing pressure, and her heart jolted as his hips ground against hers, pressing her back into the giving sand. She opened her eyes, the sky dizzily spinning into view. Her lashes felt weighted and she suddenly realised she was doing most of the kissing, Rick enjoying the novelty of feeling her tongue rubbing against his. Reluctantly she eased back, seeing the dark glaze of his gaze searching the delicate planes of her face. Her mouth had a sultry, pouting look to it.

He traced the lower curve with his thumb. 'Dynamite,' he whispered, as much trapped by the mysteries of her sexuality as she was. Unlike her, he knew exactly what he wanted to do about such heady enchantment. His gaze dropped to the curve of her breast, and with a brief economy of movement he brushed the cotton aside to display the rigid peak.

'No.' A sudden flash of panic made reality zoom back into focus.

Her body twisted as his mouth descended, the nip of his teeth making her rear against him like a wildcat. Help came from an unexpected source. A cold wave washed over both of them, destroying the world of sexual intimacy and conflict.

'Hell.' Rick Cameron pushed himself up, laughing, and grabbed hold of her, fishing her spluttering out of the foaming sea. 'That's a new line. Did the sea move for you, darling?' Viewing her features, he could see that her temper was back and she wasn't amused.

'You...' her voice was loaded with feeling '... are the most unspeakable man I've ever met.'

'You seemed to quite like me a few moments ago. Or do unspeakable men usually get to make love to you?'

'That was...' She was lost for words.

'What?' He pretended to be curious.

'...shock.' She gave him a dismissive look and headed off towards the cliff path, her progress slowed down by the sand clinging to her wet shoes and jeans. Some shock, she acknowledged, aware of his detestable presence behind her. She couldn't believe how much she had suffered at the hands of one man. Ever since she had had the misfortune to meet him he had been taking her over, making her do things that weren't quite sensible. When he was around she didn't trust herself an inch. It wasn't even as if she liked him. There was just that feeling of affinity, as if she'd known him forever. It made hitting him when he maddened her and kissing him when he turned on the charm so damned easy. No one else had ever made her behave in such a childish or passionate manner.

'I'd get down off my high horse.' His voice came from behind her. 'You'll need my help before we get to the top.'

Sweet heaven, was there no respite from his tormenting presence? Stoically she approached the path, to find its entrance barred by a steep, slippery slope of seaplaned rock. Turning, green eyes sparking, she gestured impatiently.

'How are we supposed to get up this?'

'Such ingratitude to the man who saved your life!'

'And bruised every inch of my body,' she retaliated swiftly.

'I thought you liked contact sports.' He moved past her, his voice distracted by his task. Pointing to what looked like a wrinkle in the rock, he said, 'Put your toe in there, lever yourself up, and you'll find a hand-hold to get up the rest of the way.'

Having severe misgivings, she did as he instructed. It took her a while to find the hand-hold and she tensed as Rick's hand pushed into the centre of her back to keep her from falling back down. Hot-cheeked, she sat down at the top of the rock, viewing him haughtily. Taking off her shoe, she tapped it against the hard surface, sending a shower of sand down over his head.

'Sorry,' she apologised with scant sincerity.

Brushing a hand over his face, he gave her a grimace of a smile. Approaching the slope, he proved his fitness by clearing it with a brief economy of movement, making her reflect that this particular star of celluloid didn't have fake muscles.

'It's a steep climb.' He moved ahead of her. 'Be careful.'

'Yes, boss,' she muttered, soon finding she needed all her breath for the ascent.

Following his tall figure, Helen reluctantly acknowledged that her preoccupied mood that day could have put her in danger had he not come along and rescued her. What she found unforgivable was the manner in which he had elicited personal information from her which she had not even divulged to her own mother.

Turning to extend a hand, he tugged her up over a particularly tricky bit, his eyes alive with the beauty of the evening and the challenge of the cliff path.

'Thank you.' She begrudgingly acknowledged his help.

His eyes ran over her, taking in the damp, salt-stained denim and dusting of sand that covered her clothes and skin.

'I suggest we keep to the damsel in distress story. No doubt we're going to offend public morality some time in the near future, but——'

'Oh!' Her outraged cry was expressive. She set off again, relieved to see that the difficult part of the climb was over and she didn't need to depend on his help.

He followed her all the way to Samhrad Taigh, his relaxed stride in stark comparison to her furious march. She closed her eyes with frustration when she saw the Land Rover announcing James Frazer's ultra-civilised presence.

'Hello, there.' The laird's greeting was light and friendly. 'Good gracious, what has happened to you?'

She found herself stumbling through the rescue story, feeling the mocking amusement from Rick Cameron as a tangible thing on the air.

'It's a good thing you were there, Rick.' The suspicion of a smile lingered around the older brother's mouth.

The hero of the hour shrugged modestly. 'Do you want some help getting out of there, James?'

'No, I won't get out. Helen will want to get changed. You should get changed too; I'll give you a lift back. I merely came to ask a favour.'

He glanced sideways in amused chiding at his brother's muttered, 'Spoilsport.'

'I wondered if you could help with the Midsummer Ceilidh,' he appealed with a winning smile. 'Sarah usually arranges it, of course, but it's far too much for her. I'd ask Cathy, but she has her own plans.'

'Yes, of course.' She was pleased to help, and her eyes widened slightly at the sudden intensification of Rick Cameron's gaze.

'Good.' James was cheerful. 'We won't keep you, then. I'll get in touch with you during the week.' Starting up the engine, he waited patiently for Rick.

'Nothing like getting off on the right foot,' Rick gibed as he passed her.

'I'm surprised you think that,' she returned sweetly, catching the brooding look he sent her with a faint frown. What was wrong with him? It was her right to feel aggrieved.

James gave her a cheery wave. Rick merely touched his fingers to his forehead in a minimalistic salute he'd probably practised for some film. Watching them go, she pondered on the stark contrast between the two brothers. Why, when James was so nice and decent, did she find Rick made the stronger and more persistent impression? It was a mystery she found all too easy to unravel. Dazedly her fingers came up to touch her mouth. Damn! Why did it have to be him? The dark desires at the edge of her dreams were beginning to break free. Taking a deep, shaken breath, she turned to the cottage to find solace in its gentle warmth.

CHAPTER FOUR

THE smell was delicious, but the thought made Helen shudder. She had inadvertently followed her nose to discover the mysteries of the haggis. Mary MacInnes had chuckled at the young woman's face as she had explained the process of cooking the pluck—the lungs, liver and heart—in the saucepan with the windpipe hanging over the edge. The windpipe, apparently, allowed the impurities to pass out.

'Fair fa' your honest sonsie face,
Great chieftain o' the puddin'-race!'

'Very funny.' Helen had escaped into the great hall, merely to be persecuted by Rick Cameron quoting Robert Burns.

'You'll have to have some—it's considered an essential part of the initiation process.'

'I'm sure.' Viewing the preparations in process in the room, she did her best to ignore him.

'A plateful of haggis and a few drams of Castealcreag, and you'll be a new woman.'

Casting him a baleful glance, she realised he was enjoying himself immensely. For some reason her presence at the castle was unwelcome to him. Perhaps he imagined what she gleaned of family life would end up featuring in the newspapers.

The hall was a magnificent setting, she acknowledged. Its arched timber roof with wooden diagonals and bosses reeked of history, so too did the massive oak table edged with the family motif of an eagle and thistle. The walls were white as snow, a plaster frieze, telling the history of the Lords of the Isles, running their length. A white marble fireplace reflected this conscious preservation of history, the designs reminiscent of the illuminations in the Book of Kells.

'Have your ambitions changed, I wonder?' A low laugh greeted her flash of curiosity. 'Or maybe it's the revenge of Clara MacSween.'

Hooked, Helen followed his disappearing back out of the hall, up the narrow steps to the north terrace. The wind was fresh and the view assaulted her senses. The sea gleamed under a golden sun, not a cloud in the sky, blue sky and blue sea stretching out into infinity.

'James likes you.' He stopped to open a small oak door, pulling out a roll of webbed rubber fencing.

'I like James. But I'm sure that's not what you meant.' Watching him, she made a frustrated sound in her throat as he deliberately removed the black vest he was wearing. His abdomen tightened, his biceps bunching as he pulled it over his head, his eyes challenging as he threw it aside to reveal an expanse of enviably tanned skin, sculpted over a body female fantasies could happily fixate on.

'Maybe it's a title with you,' he suggested provocatively. 'You've caused a stir in our small population— none of the ''wee lassies'' hold a candle to you. I wouldn't get too comfortable in the castle, though; I have plans for you that don't involve sharing you with my brother.'

Knowing he enjoyed her anger, she forced herself to play it cool. 'Let me reassure you, Roderick: I have no designs whatsoever, on either of you.' Reaching out, she stroked one negligent finger down his chest. 'Perhaps you should stop building your body and give your mind a chance. Then it might raise its thoughts above gutter level occasionally.'

'Live in the frigid realms you aspire to, you mean?' he enquired silkily. 'I prefer the heat.'

A deadlock of mutual hostility took hold as green eyes met hazel in a fiery conflagration. An embarrassed cough broke into the battle and Andy Frazer appeared, pointing at the fencing to explain his appearance.

'Er—ready to do that now, Rick?'

'Why not? You'll have to amuse yourself for a while, darling; I'm going to be busy.'

Giving him a speaking look, she stalked past him. For someone who suspected her of the darkest motives for being on Cladach, he went out of his way to suggest there was more between them than there actually was. She hadn't forgotten that crack about staying for breakfast! It would serve him right if she did blow the whistle on him to the Press. If the action wouldn't have unpleasant consequences for herself she would be sorely tempted.

Returning to the hall, she discovered that the folk band had arrived. They had a repertoire of ballads as well as the musical skills to play the reels and jigs necessary for a ceilidh. The Brothers of Somerled were a popular band, she realised with a shock, not restricted to the far reaches of the Highlands. She had expected the ceilidh to entertain the locals only with a few additional relatives from the neighbouring islands. She might go undetected, but how Rick Cameron expected to, with the amount of exposure the Midsummer Ceilidh would bring, she failed to guess.

An hour later the table was groaning with food. There were great dishes of traditional fare—salmon, herring, the obligatory haggis, seafood arranged temptingly on huge silver platters, cold meats, enormous pork pies— and it was hard to imagine it all being eaten. Every guest appeared to add to the table's burden. Dozens of bottles of Castealcreag whisky appeared to be in evidence, and there was a discreet bar if anyone had the affrontery to prefer anything else. Helen had never liked whisky very much, preferring a glass of wine to heavy spirits.

Disappearing to get changed, she had been offered the use of Sarah's room. She was surprised to find Sarah Frazer still in occupation when she got there, and stood back, not wishing to intrude.

'Och, come in. I'm resting. Is everything done?'

'Yes. The guests have started to arrive.' Helen studied her apprehensively. 'You look a little pale...'

'I'm fine.' The older woman patted her stomach apologetically. 'It's just the heat and being pregnant. The bathroom's through there.' She pointed towards one of the doors. 'There's a shower if you prefer it to a bath.'

'Thank you.' Helen had found it hard to get past Sarah Frazer's reserve. She didn't encourage any depth of warmth in their acquaintance. Helen suspected that she would have to live on Cladach many years before Sarah Frazer considered her a neighbour.

'Andy tells me you've been arguing with Rick.' Helen looked around, startled, as she paused on the threshold of the bathroom. 'Be careful of his temper, Helen. James refused to let him build a hotel here and look what happened to him. Rick got into one of his filthy tempers and crashed the car he was driving. As you can see, James was the one to come off worst.'

Helen looked appalled. 'You're saying he crashed on purpose?'

Sarah waved her hand dismissively. 'I'm saying that, in one of his furies, he can behave very irresponsibly. He doesn't like being refused things. I can see you're attracted to him, but for some reason of your own you prefer to fight it rather than give in. That could put you in danger. If he wants you, and senses you want him, the word "no" will mean nothing to him.' She viewed the younger woman critically. 'You're rather a godsend, not being an islander; he can have an affair with you without arousing clan censure.'

Helen found Sarah Frazer's revelations rather disconcerting. The laird's sister dismissed her by closing her eyes, and she went into the bathroom, not knowing quite what to believe. Andy Frazer had intimated that Rick's return had had to do with his brother's being unwell and his sister's being near to childbirth. It was hard to believe that his brother-in-law's loyalty and James Frazer's obvious affection were directed towards such an unstable character. Even Cathy and Mary MacInnes seemed to regard the return of their exile with a lightening of spirits. Another disturbing fact was Sarah's assumption that she was attracted to her brother. It made her feel about as transparent as a shop window.

She had wondered what to wear for such a traditional occasion. Rick had casually asked if she was to wear a kilt, which she had interpreted as setting her up for a fall. Tartan, she knew, was differentiated according to clan. Andy Frazer had taken her aside and told her that it was an informal occasion and that the young people usually wore whatever they pleased.

Helen chose a light colourful Indian print two-piece that buttoned down the front. A silver necklace with an assortment of semi-precious stones adorned her neck, silver earrings and bracelets finishing off her outfit. Drawing her hair back from her face, she used a scarf that matched her dress to tie it back. Ceilidhs, she had heard, were hot and hectic, and she intended to keep cool. Viewing herself in the mirror, she wasn't displeased with the result.

Sarah Frazer had gone when she went out into the bedroom, and Helen couldn't help feeling relieved. She didn't want to be forced into taking sides between the different factions in the Frazer family. She hadn't lived on the island long enough to judge how the changes Rick apparently favoured would affect island life. Sarah, she guessed, would be happy to make up her mind for her.

Returning to the music and merriment, Helen was soon involved in the laughing throng. Fiona MacSween had not been without friends and other distant relatives. All seemed eager to make Helen's acquaintance. Rick, she discovered, had decided to man the bar, serving everything but the ubiquitous Castealcreag.

Pouring her a glass of chilled white wine, he leant on the counter. 'Enjoying yourself?'

'Yes.' Her eyes shone brightly, her cheeks faintly pink from exertion. Rick Cameron, she noted, had his hair slicked back and was wearing dark glasses. 'You look like an Italian waiter.'

'I'm a man of many parts.' He treated her to a sleazy grin, which made her chuckle.

'So you're disguising yourself.'

'Keeping a low profile,' he agreed. 'Unlike some.'

She became flustered at that. It had never occurred to her to hide herself, and she realised why he had appeared so disgruntled by her agreement to help organise the Midsummer Ceilidh.

'As you've pointed out, my programme isn't networked here.' She made a brave recovery. The truth of the matter was that she intended to live on Cladach and she didn't wish to spend her days in hiding. The Press interest would soon die when a new candidate was presented for the consumer programme; then she would be yesterday's news. The fact that she had now become entwined in the Rick Cameron disappearance story was his problem, although she did feel a bit selfish for not looking at it from his point of view.

'Your face may not have been immediately recognisable to islanders a month ago, but if you want to have a look at the front page of nearly every tabloid you'll find that Michael Burton has announced you've got the job and has sent a plea to the nation to leave no stone unturned until you're found and acquainted with the fact.'

Helen blanched, her mouth forming on a silent refusal. Crooking a finger to invite her behind the bar,

Rick Cameron picked up a sheaf of newsprint, only too happy to provide the proof needed.

'But my mother would have called...' She broke off, wondering just how wily Moira Howard could be in pursuit of publicity.

'You would have thought so, wouldn't you?' Rick watched her leaf through the newspapers with a deep-bitten scepticism. 'I like the one in the bikini; I think I'll pin that up next to my bed.'

'Oh, God,' she groaned, casting him a murderous look. 'That was taken on the beach at some holiday resort. I don't pose for girlie shots, if that's what you're trying to insinuate...'

'We all have to work.' He pretended to understand.

The hectic Scottish reel being danced to with enthusiasm thumped around them as she held on to the vestiges of her temper.

'Not everyone goes to such extremes to achieve their ambitions, Mr Cameron.'

'I suppose your viewing figures centre around your diction,' he retaliated flippantly, taking off the dark glasses to view her more clearly. 'Let's face it, darling, if you put a bag over your head no one would bother to watch.'

'Unless they wanted to go on holiday,' she gritted, referring to the holiday programme that had built her following. 'You're not totally without a pretty-boy image yourself. Admittedly, you can act——'

'Thanks.' He pretended to be flattered by her magnanimity, his eyes black in the dim light.

'But I've seen publicity shots of you that are far more sexually provocative than that.' She slapped at the offending newspaper.

'With me, it comes naturally,' he boasted, herding her into a corner of the bar. 'What I want to know, sweetheart, is why, when you pretend to be so shy of publicity, you should reveal yourself to nearly two hundred people the very day your devious face is splashed over every popular daily.'

'I didn't know anything about the newspapers.' She tried to push him back but failed, her eyes flickering nervously over his lean features. 'I want to live here; why should I refuse a perfect opportunity to meet people?'

'Why the hell do you think?' he roared. 'I'm here, you're here, we were on the train together, and we spent the night at Mallaig. Michael Burton has posted you as a missing person; when the Press catch up, which they will, their pieces of gold will strain even island loyalties, and they're going to poke about for anything and everything they can use. I don't want my family exposed to that. It's never been a problem until you turned up!'

She laughed at the thought that she might blemish his reputation. 'What do you want me to do—make a decent man out of you? We'll say we're just good friends, although we'll blow our cover if anyone gets within a hundred yards of us...' Then the thought occurred to her that the romantic entanglement wasn't what concerned Rick Cameron. His image was that of a dedicated actor with a great deal of artistic integrity. The bad boy of Cladach, exiled at sixteen, rumoured to have crashed his car in a fit of temper, seriously injuring his brother, would certainly tarnish that image.

He coloured under his tan at her sudden perception of the underlying problem, his jaw tightening. 'So you know. I wonder how much?'

'You have my word, I won't pass on anything I know about you or your family, Rick.' She touched his arm, something in his haunted expression arousing her compassion. The muscles under his skin were hard and taut, his eyes tormented when they fixed hers in a searching fever.

'Can I have a pint of lager?' a voice broke between them, shattering the wall of raw emotion separating them from the rest of the ceilidh.

'Go and enjoy yourself,' Rick urged her, slipping on the dark glasses. 'You can't do any more damage now—most of them are drunk. Another half-hour and they won't recognise their own grandmothers.'

Helen found that her mood had sobered considerably, and was unable to contemplate joining the festivities. There was a small bus available to those wanting to leave, with a driver hired to make several trips as soon as the number made it viable. Moving towards the great oak doors, she was stopped by Andy Frazer.

'Have you seen Sally?' He looked worried. 'She's not in our room.'

'No.' She couldn't remember seeing Sarah Frazer all evening. 'It's a bit noisy; perhaps she's resting somewhere quiet.'

'Will you help me look?'

'Yes, of course,' she agreed readily.

'I'll check this floor. Will you check the terraces, Helen?'

Nodding, she made for the narrow staircase that led to the north terrace where Rick Cameron had been putting up the fencing earlier that day. Coloured lights had been strung up to give it a fairy-tale quality. The fence had put the turreted walls out of bounds which, judging by the fervour of island ceilidhs, was a wise precaution.

It didn't take her long to find the missing woman; she was sitting in a chair, bent double. Helen swallowed drily as the woman jerked with a spasm of pain.

'Sarah!' She rushed forward. 'Are you all right...?' No, she wasn't, it was obvious.

Rick appeared at the top of the stairs and Helen breathed a sigh of relief.

'I think she's having—er—contractions,' she gibbered.

'Go and get Andy. Tell him to find Martha McCellan.' Getting down on his haunches, he framed his sister's face. 'Sally? Sally, how often do the pains come?'

Skipping backwards, Helen's last sight of Rick Cameron and his sister confused her again. Whatever his misdemeanours, Rick did care for his family. He was gently talking to the woman, who was gripping his hands tightly.

Inside the noise was deafening. She pushed through a crowd of revellers to almost fall into James Frazer's arms. It was a good thing he was standing near a pillar, otherwise she would have knocked him over.

'I think Sally's having the baby. She's out on the north terrace with Rick,' she gasped. 'He said to fetch Martha McCellan.'

James nodded, looking worried. 'I'll see to that. Tell Andy.'

She went off to search the lower floor for Sarah's missing husband, hearing the music stop and the requested woman summoned. Everything seemed to happen quickly after that. She informed Andy Frazer, who went white. James's wheelchair was brought and Rick disappeared to bring the helicopter down as close as he could to the castle.

Mary MacInnes came to stand at Helen's shoulder, watching the helicopter lift into the sky, the blades slicing into the warm, velvety night and creating a rush of air.

'It's a good thing Rick was here,' she commented grimly. 'I doubt it will be an easy birth—Martha looked very grave.'

The guests decanted in busloads, and Helen, who doubted she would sleep, helped Mary clear away the debris. She collected a mass of paper plates, putting them into black plastic bags, and then began to collect glasses.

At four o'clock in the morning they were sitting drinking a cup of tea, glasses gleaming around them, when James limped down into the kitchen.

'They've reached the hospital. The baby was in an awkward position but the doctor has managed to turn it. Fingers crossed, everything should go well from now on.'

'Och, that's good news!' Mary MacInnes's tired face was transformed by a relieved smile.

Helen let out a long breath. 'Would you like a cup of tea, James?'

'I would.' He regarded her warmly. 'It's very good of you to stay, Helen. Thank you for all your help.'

She smiled, a faint frown creasing her brow. 'James, did you see the newspapers...?'

'Yes.' His eyes twinkled. 'What will you do? You wanted the job, did you not?'

'I thought so at the time.' Her frown deepened. 'I think I'll have to go back to London just to settle the publicity. Otherwise the Press will find their way here and disturb Rick's privacy.'

James nodded thoughtfully. 'I doubt Rick cares that much for himself, but there are a few family matters we would prefer remained private. Nothing too sensational in this day and age, but no one particularly likes to have their history laid bare for all eyes to see.'

'No,' she agreed solemnly. Remembering the Gary Chambers incident, she was all too aware of how innocent facts could be blown up out of all proportion. The car crash involving the Frazer brothers would make uncomfortable reading if Sarah or any of the other islanders revealed the circumstances that had preceded it.

'I'll phone my agent in the morning—later this morning,' she qualified, glancing at the clock.

'You're welcome to spend what is left of the night at Castealcreag,' James offered. 'Mary, would you be kind enough to show Helen to one of the guest rooms?'

'Of course. I expect we'll both sleep easier knowing that Sarah and the baby are all right.'

She was grateful to accept the offer. Three hours' hard work had worn off the tension created by Sarah Frazer's abrupt departure from the Midsummer Ceilidh. She barely noticed the décor of the room she was offered, shedding her skirt and top, slipping between the cool sheets with a grateful sigh.

In the fog of sleep, she heard the beating blades of the helicopter. Slipping in and out of dreams, she dreamt she was crying, looking for someone. At first it was her father, but he disappeared along a complex network of streets and alleys. She was lost and crying. There was someone else there too, but she couldn't turn around to see. She wasn't ready to give up the search. The dream repeated itself endlessly and she woke up confused, with Rick's name on her lips.

Blinking and frowning at the unfamiliar room, Helen shook herself free from the remnants of her dream. It would have to be a nightmare to have Rick Cameron in it, she decided, but the feeling of being enmeshed with the man persisted.

She studied her surroundings drowsily. The room was muted blue and grey and had an androgynous quality to it, necessary for a room offered to both male and female guests. White linen pillowcases with the embroidered family motif and coverlets made out of intricate patchwork in white, blue and grey were surprisingly timeless.

Exploring, she found a small shower had been added, using an area which might possibly have been a dressing-room in the past. Pale blue and white towels nested on a heated rail, and after her shower she wrapped one around herself, finding a plastic-wrapped toothbrush waiting in the wall cabinet.

'They think of everything,' she murmured. She was about to dress when the door of her room opened and an unshaven and heavy-eyed Rick Cameron came in with a breakfast tray.

'Get out!' she shrieked, but the sound came out as a husky squeak. He took no notice, kicking the door shut with his foot.

'Sally had a little girl. Seven pounds something or other. They're both fine.'

'Oh, good.' The news still didn't give him a right to come into her bedroom without knocking, and she noted, incensed, that he had put two cups on the tray, which suggested he intended to stay. 'She wanted to discharge herself and come back. Andy discovered his backbone and refused to allow it. I said I'd go back on Wednesday and she'd have to wait until then.' Pushing restless fingers through his hair, he gave her a brooding look. 'She said she was sorry for what she'd said about me. Does that make any sense to you, or was it just the stuff they gave her to get over the pain?'

Helen avoided his eyes guiltily. She didn't wish to reveal the context of the conversation she'd had with Sarah. He had a way of discovering her secrets that left her feeling extremely vulnerable.

An infuriating smile curled his mouth. Helen could almost believe he had read her thoughts!

'If you've got over your maidenly modesty I'll pour the tea.'

'I'd rather you left.' She kept hold of the towel, wishing it were a little larger. 'If you want company I'll join you downstairs.'

'I want to talk.' Dark lashes lifted to reveal eyes the colour of woody glades.

'I've already decided to go to London and face the Press there.' She attempted to shorten the discussion, not liking the way his gaze had begun a lazy survey of her legs.

'Will you stay?' He smiled at her indignation at his liberty-taking.

'I don't know. I suppose I'm only getting the job because awkward questions have been asked about my pulling out of the race.'

Rick Cameron shrugged. 'I'd watch.'

'I suppose you want me off the island.' She fired up, suddenly catching on to his motive. 'God, you're devious. Last night I was a talentless calendar girl; this morning you can't wait for me to relaunch my career.'

Watching her rage with insulting calm, he closed in, with a practised familiarity in the way he invaded her space that made her hackles rise.

'You're always crowding me,' she accused him, her hold on the towel feeling even less secure the closer he came. His fingers gripped the rounded curve of her shoulders, his lean face inches from hers.

'You worry me,' he purred, his breath warm against her lips. 'Faced with a guy like Burton, all you can do is run. Do you think he wants you any less because you've got a little dangerous? It just makes you more of a prize.'

'Your concern is touching,' she retaliated, but her eyes showed her confusion. One minute he seemed to be urging her back, the next, warning her of the dangers she faced.

'My concern is territorial.' The news that Helen was going back to London to face the Press had pleased Rick Cameron. It took the heat off Cladach. The fact that she might become entangled in the web of the lecherous Michael Burton was rather less appealing.

'What did you do? Let those beautiful green eyes make promises you couldn't keep? Some women tease because they know that beyond the glitter is dross. But you're not like that, Helen; you're frightened of the power in your body, frightened it will make you its slave.'

Helen met his eyes in scornful denial, but his smoky, sensual appraisal made her swallow drily. She had to escape... quickly! The towel rubbed abrasively against her skin; she wanted rid of it, and... What she wanted made her try to push past him with an inarticulate murmur of panic.

Something happened. The towel jerked. She became caught up in its folds and fell to the floor in an ungainly heap.

Laughing hatefully, Rick attempted to disentangle her, and ducked as she aimed a slap at his head and then grabbed a tuft of his hair.

'You stood on my towel,' she accused hotly.

'Sounds like a good idea.' He winced at the pull against his scalp. 'But it was an accident.'

'You . . . !' Helen glared up at him as he forced the offending hand back on to the carpet, shaking his head as if to ease the sting. 'I hope it hurt,' she gibed childishly.

'Looking at you makes it better.'

Helen realised with a shock that the towel had slipped free of her upper body and her breasts were bared to his view. And he was looking. Dear lord, how he was looking!

Helen found the words of anger trapped in her throat. The memory of the moments on the beach made her pulses race. 'My concern is territorial'—that was the way he was looking at her. As if she was something rare he wanted to possess. He trapped her in his desires and somehow managed to ignite her own. Her eyes widened to take in his dark form as he let go of her hands and let one of his hands stroke down her arm.

'Poor, weak flesh,' he murmured, mocking her. 'Held back by a frigid mind.'

'I am not frigid . . .' The words whispered from her lips, her senses unbearably aware of the trail of his fingers. The tingle coming from the inner hollow of her elbow seemed to ripple over her body in a feather of sensation that tormented for more.

'Prove it.' The challenge was soft, and the air between them sizzled with sexual awareness. His hand continued the light caress, brushing over her shoulder, running lightly up and down her arm. 'Or would you rather go back and play office games with your new boss?'

Before she could form a protest to his unjust prediction Helen found her mouth firmly possessed, her mind in chaos and her body curving to his as if it had suddenly discovered the purpose of its design. Helen couldn't believe the way all her protective anger and years of abstinence could melt away when confronted with this man. He made her want things she had never wanted before. She just knew she wasn't going to stop him kissing her and felt appalled and excited at the same time.

Taken straight from a stolen kiss on the beach to the demand of full-blooded adult sexuality was like diving into a deep pool with the advantage of only one swimming lesson. Helen found herself sinking lower and lower into the mysterious depths, floundering helplessly as Rick Cameron's mouth explored and moulded her own, her lips trembling against his, her breath taken and given until she felt as if he breathed for them both.

Her eyes briefly opened in shock when his mouth travelled over her cheek to bury into her throat, biting gently, her wild response as she wound her arms around his neck making the pressure of their bodies almost painful. She could feel his heart thundering in his chest, his breathing shallow and rapid, the material of his scarlet T-shirt warm and slightly abrasive against the hardened peaks of her nipples. She must have protested about the irritation because he let her go, dragging off his T-shirt, pulling her closer again with possessive intensity.

'Better,' he murmured into her mouth, the heat of his skin and the tickle of his soft body hair making her surfacing awareness dive back down into the sensual depths once more. His tongue pushed impatiently between her lips, her mouth relaxing to take the impact, her hands tightening on the hard bone of his shoulder as he lifted

her and eased her on to the bed. Their mouths still fused
together, he pulled the towel free before inserting an imperative thigh between hers, one dark, sinewy hand
sweeping up her body to grasp her breast.

His mouth dragged free of hers, roaming hungrily over
her shoulders, before exploring her upper chest, his hand
tightening on her breast until the rosy crest screamed for
the rough lash of his tongue. When it came Helen's body
arched, his name a soft plea on her lips, her golden hair
tumbled around her flushed cheeks, the abrasive denim-
covered thigh between hers dominating the soft upthrust
of her pelvis but failing to satisfy the growing ache there.

Driven by buried instincts, Helen's hand slid from his
shoulder, down over his bicep to the hair-roughened skin
of his forearm. Her fingers sought his, drawing them
away from her breast and down over her ribs to her
stomach.

Rick lifted his head and smiled into her eyes, but his
gaze was electric. 'If you were Helen of Troy...' he spoke
huskily, watching for her response as his fingers stroked
gently over her belly to the silky down guarding her loins
'...I would never have left the harbour.'

Helen shuddered, her purely female cry arousing a
similar need in her male partner. If anyone had told her
that she, Helen Howard, was capable of undressing a
man without a moment's hesitation, she wouldn't have
believed it. But her fingers negotiated the zip fastening
to his jeans, and she pushed the material down his lean
thighs, stroking his skin as she did so.

Rick possessed her with a hard thrust of his body that
made her cry out in distress. He gentled considerably,
his mind a long way behind his body in its perception.
The hot tide of passion engulfed her once more, al-
lowing her to accept the growing storm driving the man
who held her. And she became part of that storm too,
revelling in the elemental forces ravaging their senses.
Lightning flowed through her, her body stretching with

the sheer love-agony of it. She feared it would destroy her, and then Rick brought her back, his lips touching hers in a feather-light kiss, as the storm shuddered through their bodies and ebbed away.

The androgynous blue-grey room swung back into focus, its muted colours bland after the vividness of touch and sensation.

Rick Cameron found himself coping with a host of very different emotions. His possessive instincts were getting totally out of control. His previous bout of self-congratulation when she had decided to go to London felt like ashes in his mouth. With her impetuous nature he didn't want her out of his sight!

Helen could hardly look at him. It must be sheer lust! She burnt with embarrassment and shame. It was doubtful whether she actually liked Rick Cameron and yet she had allowed him to make her body his own.

'Helen?' His brooding gaze took in the evidence of their lovemaking, one lazy brown finger touching a faint mark on her neck. 'I suppose there's a good reason why you didn't ask me to protect you?' he queried, his tone dry. Watching the shocked realisation darken her eyes, he sighed. 'That's what I thought.'

CHAPTER FIVE

'SO LET'S talk about it!' Rick Cameron emptied the contents of the suitcase out on to the bed to Helen's choked cry of rage.

'Are you worried about your reputation again?' she sniped, trying to push past him to re-pack her things.

Rick glared at her, finding her eminently frustrating and desirable, dressed as she was for travelling in pale denims and a chunky-knit white jumper decorated with pale pastel butterflies. Her hair was brushed back, hanging loosely around her shoulders, streaks of burnished gold visible from his standpoint, almost on top of her, against the darker hair below. 'If you'd told me—— '

'You didn't give me a chance.' She felt her cheeks grow scarlet. Pushing him, she managed to get back to her suitcase, gritting her teeth as he took hold of her shoulders and turned her to him.

'Look, I can't change what happened. I mean, it's not every day of the week——'

'You meet that rare creature, a virgin,' she supplied acidly. 'I'm sorry I didn't prepare you for the shock.'

Frowning, he searched her troubled features and let his breath out expressively. 'I knew you were trouble the minute I set eyes on you. Light the fuse, and pow! Sometimes it's good, other times you get burnt.'

'Is that your charming, colonial way of saying thanks, but no, thanks, because if it is——'

'I don't run from my responsibilities, Helen.' His voice hardened, as if he was getting tired of her rages.

78

'Well, I don't wish to be a responsibility of yours. Consider yourself absolved.'

Digging his hands into his pockets, Rick regarded her from between narrowed lashes. 'What are you going to do about the job? Take it?'

'That hardly concerns you.' She was prim.

'I suggest you keep your relationship with Burton strictly businesslike.'

She had begun to pack her things and looked up at that, anger kindling in the depths of her eyes.

He came close on his way to the door. 'If you don't, you'll find the kind of publicity you're so eager to avoid.' Pure menace emanated from every pore as he transfixed her gaze.

Helen remained silent. Soon she would be rid of his tormenting presence. There was something in him she didn't want to challenge.

The journey south was long and uneventful. Glad that the cloak and dagger business was over with, Helen returned to the house she shared with her mother for a night's rest before the Press conference the next morning.

It had been relatively easy to push the subject of Rick Cameron out of her mind when she'd been travelling. In the peaceful environs of Hampstead it was another matter. What had happened to her? She had known Rick was a threat from the moment they had met, so why hadn't she screamed blue murder when he had come into her room? Why couldn't she have said no to him? It made her protests look like coy foreplay.

Moira Howard regarded her daughter shrewdly. 'Has someone ruffled your feathers? You look different.'

Reddening, Helen wondered if her brief descent into the realms of sensuality had actually changed her in some way. Keeping her poise with considerable effort, she gestured across the room to the pile of tabloids her mother had collected. 'I was surprised you didn't get in touch about those.'

'Oh, I thought you'd see them,' her parent replied airily. 'Besides, I was away for a few days on a trip to Dorset. Gilbert's getting rather romantic in his old age. We had a lovely time.' Gilbert Locke was her mother's long-suffering admirer. He had been a friend when John Howard had been alive and had only recently put himself forward as a prospective partner.

'He's been in love with you for years,' Helen teased, grateful to have the onus off her own romantic entanglements.

Moira Howard smiled, clearly pleased by the thought. Pouring some tea into the china cups she had assembled, she passed her daughter a cup, her eyes curious as they rested on Helen's golden beauty.

'Will you take the job? Whatever the problem was appears to be ironed out—they can hardly back out now.'

Helen looked as pensive as she felt. A month ago she would have refused the olive branch offered by Michael Burton with a great deal of satisfaction. Rick's dramatic entry into her life had made her a little more cautious. Cladach was his territory. She had received a warm welcome, but she was shrewd enough to know that if she incurred Frazer disapproval she would find it very difficult to do more than exist on the island. There were also the limitations of the shop. At the moment she was in the process of clearing out and updating the stock on offer. She was temporarily occupied sorting out regular delivery dates and becoming familiar with the durability and practicality of certain lines, but this was the task of months rather than years. She needed an outlet for her energy and creativity and the journalistic elements of the consumer programme had appealed to her. She had spent too long fronting beautifully photographed resorts. Investigative journalism was her home ground, and this programme offered her the chance to hone her skills. She had had enough of putting her eggs in one basket. She could use her TV career and life on Cladach as counterweights to balance against each other when the going got tough.

'I'm meeting the producer tomorrow,' she revealed, aware of Moira Howard's smile of satisfaction.

Her agent Terri Donovan was going to be present, so she hoped that would circumvent any renewed attempts by Michael Burton to put her in an embarrassing position. 'When I've discussed terms I'll attend the Press conference, and that, hopefully, will be the end of it.'

'It's been quite fun. I'm sure Gilbert and I were followed to Dorset.' Her mother viewed the whole thing in a light-hearted fashion, and Helen couldn't help smiling.

'There's a reception in the evening should I sign the contract. Do you want to go? You could bring Gilbert.'

'Lovely.' Moira Howard enjoyed such occasions even if her daughter did seem to find that side of the business totally unnecessary. 'Helen...is everything all right? I hope I'm not one of those mothers daughters find it impossible to talk to. You are twenty-five, and I'm reasonably broad-minded.'

Helen's lovely face was a picture of perplexity. 'I...it's the job, I expect. I'm all right really.'

'Oh.' Her mother sounded ominous. 'Poor Helen. Love you can't plan. Is he the forceful type?'

'Who?' she fenced ineffectively, desperate to keep off the subject of Rick Cameron. Avoiding her mother's eyes, she stood up. 'I suppose I'd better go to bed.' Helen wasn't looking forward to her meeting with Michael Burton, and it showed, distracting Moira Howard momentarily from the speculation on her daughter's love-life.

'Don't worry. Terri Donovan will make sure you get a good deal. What have you decided to do about the cottage? Will you sell it?'

'No.' Her firmness on the subject made her mother blink. 'If I accept Metro's offer I'll get help with the

shop. I'm keeping Samhrad Taigh. I need somewhere to
get away from it all.'

'Does this man live on the island?'

'No, not really.' Helen's thoughts were a long way off,
with the sound of the gulls, the mournful curlew and
bright yellow of wild gorse. She didn't realise how much
she had given away.

Giving her a long look, Moira Howard kept her peace.
'You must be a throwback. My mother was glad to get
away, and, I must say, the attraction beats me.'

Helen grinned and they parted with a warm,
'Goodnight.'

Helen chose her outfit carefully the next morning. She
decided on a deep mauve wrap-around top, a belt to
match with ornate silver buckle, and a skirt that picked
up the colour amid a background of charcoal and amber.
The day was cool and she pulled on a pair of light
summer boots, chunky silver jewellery adorning her ears
and wrists. Putting her hair up in a French plait, she
sprayed on some of her favourite Chanel perfume.
Grabbing a pale mauve corduroy jacket, she hitched it
over her shoulder, and obeyed the toot on the horn from
her agent Terri Donovan.

'Glad to see you back in the land of the living.' Her
agent was tongue-in-cheek. 'You've had my phone tied
up all week.'

'Sorry.' Helen was monosyllabic, and Terri's eyes cast
upwards as if asking for divine guidance.

'Well, you look gorgeous. What have you been doing
with yourself?'

'Resting.' She used the old cliché. 'Terri, I don't want
to be tied up in a mass of mindless PR work. Keep it to
the minimum, will you?'

'Naturally.' Terri Donovan inspected her client with
proprietorial interest. Red-haired and dressed in maroon,
she was flamboyant and feisty. Helen Howard was a bit

of a mystery to her. She reminded Terri of a Mediterranean sea, where that fascinating transition between blue and green was struck by sunlight. There was a peculiar transcendence between coolness, warmth and languidity mixed with puritanical strength which was quite formidable and infinitely misleading. Instinct told her she'd got a winner, but why eluded her.

Helen was immersed in an inner perusal of why she had taken flight in such a manner. It wasn't as if men hadn't pressed their advances before. Had she felt threatened by Michael Burton because she'd been afraid she might submit? The thought occupied her and then she dismissed it. Perhaps she had reached a time in her life when the demands of nature were too hard to ignore. She had decided that her personal ambition would not sacrifice her inner conviction that emotion should precede commitment, and yet she wondered if love lay behind her relationship with Rick Cameron. Certainly he galvanised her senses; it would be pointless to deny that. Yet what did she know of him? He was a Frazer who had left his home and sought fame and fortune in Hollywood. He reputedly had a temper that was dangerous and a personality that, while addictive, was oppressively encroaching. She needed him and feared him at the same time.

Entering the familiar glass doors of Metro Television, Helen was greeted by the receptionist, who manufactured an ecstatic welcome that was all lip-gloss and teeth. She was immediately whisked up to the programme producer's office. His door was painted a metallic blue, picking up the stripe in the discreet but ubiquitous carpet that paraded Metro's colours throughout the whole building.

Michael Burton was the golden boy of Metro TV, figuratively and literally. An angel without a halo as far as Helen was concerned. She faced his plastic welcome and tried to assume a polite expression. He had immaculately groomed blond hair that persistently curled, baby-blue eyes and a mouth that just missed the rosebud appellation. He wore a grey checked suit with a quiet tie, his smile just a little too fulsome for all the trouble Helen Howard had caused him.

'Wonderful,' he greeted Helen, kissing her cheek with assumed warmth. 'Where have you been, darling? We've been positively frantic.'

'On holiday.' Helen remained cool, deciding he was everything she disliked.

'Somewhere fairly remote, obviously.' His eyes sharpened at the flicker of her lashes. 'Never mind, you're here now. Terri,' he acknowledged the woman watching the exchange. 'How are you?'

'Fine. Just recovering from being invisible.' The last crack was in an undertone, and Helen found her mouth curling into a smile.

Michael Burton hastily glanced from one to the other and, deciding they were too formidable to break down as a team, he got down to business.

The TV company wanted Helen to host the show while other journalists did the real groundwork. This she refused, and a compromise was hammered out where she and one of the other presenters would take turns playing anchorman.

'We need your face every week,' Michael Burton stressed. 'The public will soak up whatever you sell them, but without your charisma the programme may flop.'

'I don't believe the public are that gullible.' Helen found him patronising in the extreme. 'If we have a good basic structure and journalists the public can identify with then I think that will be the recipe for success.'

'What about money?' Terri Donovan cut in. 'As you've pointed out yourself, Helen draws the crowds...'

The haggling continued, Helen withdrawing from the bartering, her mind wandering back to Cladach. Gales were forecast for the Hebrides. She would still rather have been there than go to the promotional evening that night.

The programme was to be called *Option Three*. It was based on the philosophy that people either accepted a bad deal, got their money back or took alternative action when the second option was frustrated. Helen was desultorily flicking through her wardrobe for an outfit for the publicity launch when her mother paraded into her bedroom in a cerise two-piece. At forty-five, she was still a very attractive woman, and the suit gave colour to her fair skin, her hair as gold as Helen's, styled in a neat bob.

'What do you think?' She twirled for her daughter's approval.

'Very chic,' Helen admired the outfit.

'What are you going to wear?'

Helen hadn't decided. Her brain had turned to cotton wool and she rather suspected the combined pressures of her lifestyle over the last month had made their mark.

'Dear me. We are on cloud nine, aren't we?' Her mother went to look through her daughter's wardrobe.

'That green thing will do.'

'This, you mean?' Her mother held up an exquisite green silk dress that foxed the eye. It was grey-blue-green, all three in different perspectives. 'Yes, this will suit you; it's suitably mystical. I hope this dream world you're in isn't permanent. I rather like you when you're being firm and decisive. It makes you less vulnerable.'

Helen accepted the dress, becoming thoughtful when her mother left to greet Gilbert, who had signalled his presence at the door. Was she safer behind that no-nonsense façade, or did she need to learn to live with her vulnerability? Most women seemed to come to terms with their emotions and, she reluctantly admitted, their desires. Hadn't she already begun to cope with the less pleasant pressures of her public life by creating a breathing-space, a place to go to relax? Cladach was beginning to feel less like an escape and more like a safety valve to relax the pressure and tensions of her work. Keeping on Samhrad Taigh would be an eminently sensible decision if it weren't for the continued threat of Rick Cameron's presence. But then, she would have to learn to deal with that too!

The party was a carbon copy of many Helen had attended. It was held in a fashionable Kensington nightclub called Babes, a special area having been cordoned off for the *Option Three* team and their guests. The champagne and caviare were abundant, the music was loud and vibrant, the colours from the lighting system and the fashion-conscious clientele vivid.

Terri Donovan appeared at Helen's shoulder, her red hair in a state of shock against an orange jump suit. Helen's agent had had a convent education and was in a constant state of rebellion against subdued colours and fitting in. She led a flamboyant lifestyle, escorted by various males equally into bizarre dress, and tried to hide the fact that she lived comfortably alone with two cats, Herbie and Mildred.

'Not too hard on the haggling front, I thought. Is somebody feeling guilty about something?' She eyed Helen closely.

'Perhaps.' Helen smiled slowly and saw confirmation written on her agent's face.

'That man is a creep. I was furious when you disappeared but, now I've had time to reflect, I think you did the right thing.'

'Thank you.' Helen took a glass of champagne off a silver tray being woven through the crowd by a smart young man in evening dress.

'Isn't it loud?' Moira Howard broke into their conversation, towing Gilbert Locke, the even-featured grey-haired man close behind her.

'Helen.' Scott Barnes, her co-presenter, came up and claimed her for a dance, a photographer appearing out of nowhere and taking a photograph no doubt destined for the morning newspapers.

The night followed the usual pattern. Helen was never short of partners but all were transitory, and if they showed a desire to stay she soon managed to detach herself without being rude. When Michael Burton came towards her Helen's eyes became hard with rejection.

'You can't refuse.' He spoke in an undertone. 'You'll make a scene. Let's let bygones by bygones; I've got the message.'

'One dance,' she stipulated, getting up and trying her best to hide her displeasure.

As luck would have it, the music, while not exactly slowing down entirely, did lose pace somewhat, which allowed a limited exchange of conversation.

'The Press are still sniffing around, wanting to know why you disappeared like that,' Michael Burton revealed, his eyes scanning the crowd, one hand resting lightly on her waist as they turned in unison to the music.

'I'll tell them I didn't like your original terms,' Helen replied sweetly to the implication that she had put him into a tight spot.

He smiled, but his eyes were unpleasant. 'Now, now, we don't want it to be one of those programmes benighted by internecine squabbles, do we?'

'We don't?' Helen was not about to be manipulated into anything she didn't like.

'Couldn't you come up with something suitably convincing? A friend in dire distress, a sick dog...anything.'

'I don't make a habit of speaking to the Press on private matters.' She stood her ground. 'And I don't intend to start now.'

Grateful when the dance ended, she made her way back to the table she shared with her mother, Gilbert and her agent. Sitting down, she sipped her champagne, feeling rather hot, only to turn to stone when she saw Rick Cameron making his way around the edge of the dance-floor. Without his dark glasses he was easily recognised, and heads were turning left, right and centre.

'Oh, no,' she murmured, which was picked up by Terri Donovan, who followed her gaze and clutched her friend's arm.

'Good God. That's Rick Cameron. What do you mean, "Oh, no"?' A sudden flash of insight made her glance from one to the other. 'I want an exclusive to run this story to every woman's magazine that will pay the readies. If you've been hiding away with...' The rest went over Helen's head; she was in a whirl of confusion. After such care avoiding publicity, what was he doing here?

That night Rick Cameron was fully prepared to be a film star. Gone were the jeans and T-shirt. He wore a soft brown suede jacket, pockets detailed on the breast, matched with a patterned shirt and chinos. The pale khaki trousers had suede detailing on the pockets and a thin leather belt that bespoke expensive design. Viewing the surrounding dinner suits and fashion victims, he felt he steered a commendable middle road.

'Will you dance with me?' His voice had an amused inflexion at Helen's astonishment.

'What? Oh...yes, all right.' Getting to her feet, she was conscious of a million eyes, not the least of which belonged to her astonished parent.

'What are you doing here?' she demanded, involved in a furtive conversation for the second time that night.

Rick regarded her with intimate warmth, drawing her into his arms, regardless of the tempo of the music. 'Aren't you pleased to see me, darling?'

'Everyone will think——' A soft kiss covered her mouth, and Helen was almost blinded by the flash from a camera. 'What are you doing?' She was too incensed to wonder at the tingling warmth he brought to her lips.

'Going public.' He brushed a kiss across her forehead. 'You are my woman, aren't you?'

'You must be joking...' She broke off, recognising one prominent member of the paparazzi edging near to them.

'You'd better not belong to anyone else.' His eyes were darkly possessive as they ran over the loveliness of her face. 'Where's this guy you're having trouble with?'

'Oh, no,' she warned urgently. 'Don't you dare. I mean it, Rick. I don't know what you're playing at, but I won't have you interfering this way!'

When the record finished he grasped her wrist firmly, leading her from the dance-floor, advancing towards the main party. Dragging her feet, she was aware of being the subject of open speculation and discreet interest from various gathered parties.

Michael Burton had watched as avidly as the rest. Rick Cameron's appearing on the scene adequately squashed any speculation there had been about his involvement with Helen. He was silently congratulating himself until the tall, impressively built actor began to head in his direction. Helen Howard was the sort of woman to bring out many aspects of a man's character, some chivalrous, others not so gentlemanly. If Cameron was her lover, as their closeness suggested, then he assumed he might have figured in their pillow talk.

With a glassy smile Michael Burton held his ground. The homing instinct of the paparazzi suggested that retreat would be well documented.

'Michael, my boss.' Helen attempted to maintain elements of civility and introduced them. 'This is Rick Cameron. He wanted to meet you.'

Michael Burton extended his hand, withering slightly at the sheer force of personality exuded by the film star.

'I don't want to shake hands. I have only one thing to say to you, Burton: if you don't want to end up front page, with a broken jaw, I advise you to keep away from Helen. Do we understand each other?'

'Yes.' Burton maintained the smile, glad that any photographs being taken were of Cameron's back view.

'Good.' Rick lost interest, turning to look down into a pair of eyes burning with green fire. 'Shall we go, sweetheart? We're going to be knee-deep in reporters if we don't go soon.'

'I think we could do with a private discussion,' she agreed, her voice stiff. 'If you'll wait a moment, I'll just say my goodbyes.'

'I'll explain later,' she halted the storm of questions about to be put to her by her mother and Terri Donovan. 'I'll see you back at the house, Mum.'

Helen stalked from the nightclub into the neon-lit darkness of the city night. To say she was angry would be light-years from the sheer fury boiling within her. Rick hailed a taxi, sitting back, relaxed, as the driver obeyed his instructions. He'd given an address in Knightsbridge.

'Are we being followed?' Helen asked frigidly, quite familiar with the antics of the Press.

'Probably.' Rick appeared to be uncaring of the possible publicity. 'What's the matter? You couldn't go on being the Miss Clean of broadcasting all your life.'

Dark and mocking, Rick Cameron regarded her concern with barely concealed impatience.

On Cladach she had been the intruder into his life, his home. Here he was carving a swath into her existence in a manner she objected to. He had exposed them both to gossip and speculation without consulting her on the matter, and had threatened Michael Burton when she considered she had already negotiated a truce with her producer.

Paying off the taxi driver, they had to walk a block until they came to the mansion apartment. Rick Cameron, despite his apparently blasé attitude to publicity, didn't want the Press camping on his doorstep and was all too aware that taxi drivers weren't above capitalising on their celebrity fares.

'My father bought this place back in the fifties, supposedly to promote Castealcreag business interests.' Passing the doorman, with whom Rick was clearly familiar, they walked up a short flight of ornately decorated staircase to the first floor. Gesturing to the elegant furnishings in the flat, he invited her to enter. 'I'm the only one who uses this. We should rent it out but it's kept for my occasional use and Sally's once-a-year shopping spree in London.'

The apartment had a faded splendour that suggested the furnishings had remained the same for some time. The lack of use no doubt accounted for the resilience of the textiles against the march of time. The walls were painted a pale lavender colour with cream paintwork, and the colours were reflected in the armchairs and rug that covered much of the floor. There were various paintings of Highland scenes, large and small, providing interest here and there, discreet bookshelves with modern paperbacks, which she assumed were Rick's, and an impressive stereo system she also attributed to him. A highly polished coal scuttle was occupied by a mass of heather and stood before a grey brick fireplace containing a pile of logs. It was undoubtedly the home of a family who spent their time looking back towards their island home.

'I've been rather stupid, haven't I?' Helen gazed around her. What she saw was a tenacious spirit. A compromise with the needs of the world but a deep-seated desire for home and all that home meant. 'You've used me as a decoy to distract the Press from your real reason for delaying the film.'

'It won't suit either of us if the Press discover Cladach.' Rick regarded her speculatively, powerful and virile among the gentleness of lavender and heather. 'And what do you know of my reasons for returning to the island? I know you've made quite a hit with some of the islanders, but I wouldn't mistake gossip for cold, hard facts.'

'Tell me the truth, then!' Helen approached him, her green eyes brilliant with challenge. 'Why have you involved me in this charade?'

Helen's slender grace distracted her companion, his gaze roaming over the golden blush the sun had given her face, the war-light in her emerald eyes and the mobile lines of her mouth. Rick Cameron couldn't subdue the glimmer of amusement when her expression became highly critical of his regard.

'It seems like a long time since we——'

'Don't you dare change the subject! And take that look out of your eyes; I know what that means.'

'You're a quick learner,' he provoked her. 'And it won't take you long to learn that wanting someone doesn't go away. It mellows and then bites at you again.' His gaze continued to strip her, and he caught her hand as it whipped towards his cheek. 'It seems as though we've played this game before. Want me to do something about all that frustration?' He twisted her arm behind her back, capturing the other wrist and imprisoning them both with one of his hands. When she went to kick him he pushed one leg between hers and unbalanced her. 'I'll let you go if you promise to be good.'

'You're totally unscrupulous,' she spat at him, the heat from his thigh awakening her traitorous senses.

'And you have a nasty temper,' he goaded her, his hazel eyes gleaming with triumph at her impotent struggles that were having a very potent effect on him.

'So have you, if rumour is to be believed.' She could have bitten out her tongue. He'd got her exactly where he wanted her and the knowledge of his victory showed in her eyes.

'And what does rumour say?' The quiet menace in his voice actually frightened her. 'I'm supposed to take after my father. He beat me black and blue before I left Cladach. Do you think violence runs in families? Is that what makes you look at me as if part of you is scared and wants to run away?'

'No...I...' Why was she denying it? He did scare her. His sheer persistence was wearing. His entry into her world in London had been something she wasn't prepared for. He was waiting now. Prepared to use his forceful personality to gain an answer. She remembered how he had taunted her that day on the beach until she had told him her reasons for leaving London. Unwilling to go through that humiliating experience again, she told him what he wanted to know.

'People say you have a dangerous temper...'

'People do?' He watched her face colour delicately as she twisted her head to the side, her golden hair hiding her profile. 'And why do they say that?' His voice was soft, but his mouth burning on the exposed skin of her shoulder made her struggle to be free. Dark excitement twisted through her; she couldn't let it happen again!

'James...' she gasped. 'The crash...it was your fault.' She didn't continue, her mouth going dry at his expression. His fingers became painful against her wrists, one hand forcing her chin up to leave her vulnerable to the fury of his gaze. His skin had gone white under the tan, his jaw rigid, a muscle moving in his lean cheek.

'You little bitch.' His voice was harsh and cold. 'Yes, I was driving. I had head injuries. I have only James's word for what happened. I can't remember a thing. And James is a nice guy, as you quite obviously appreciate, so I don't know the truth of it. One thing I do know: I've loved and admired my brother all my life and, if I had any choice in the matter, I'd be the one suffering the pain.'

Letting her go abruptly, he swept up car keys from one of the small tables. 'I'll take you home, if you're prepared to take the risk.' His tone derided her.

'I'd rather get a taxi.' She didn't apologise for her words. His anger was her only defence. If he softened and forgave her she didn't trust herself to leave before morning. It was a terrible feeling to be so far out of control.

She went to the phone in his apartment. 'I'm not worried about your driving,' she offered, determined to keep up hostilities. 'But, in the interests of my publicity, I don't mind being seen leaving your apartment.'

'For your cosy single bed in Hampstead,' he sneered.

'It seems strangely attractive,' she agreed, her chin lifting proudly. 'We have a fictional romance created by you in the minds of the Press. I have no intention of having any sort of relationship with you!'

'If you cast your mind back you'll realise you passed "Go" several moves back.' Rick approached her, taking the receiver and dialling a cab firm he was familiar with. 'I'll ride back with you. If you got mugged or worse I'd have that lain at the door of my famous temper, and there's only so much guilt I can handle.'

Helen settled for giving him a filthy look and sat down at the other side of the room to wait for the taxi to arrive. They were back where they had started, at war with that fine sexual tension between them that had demands all of its own. The evening ended with him seeing her to the door of her home.

'Goodnight, Helen of Hampstead; I'll be in touch.'

Perfectly aware of the degree of demotion from Helen of Troy, she said goodbye in an icy manner, knowing that that wouldn't be the end of things between them. 'Aunt Fi, what have you got me into?' she murmured as the cab drew away from the kerb. The twitch of the curtain caught her eye and she sighed deeply. The evening wasn't over yet—she still had to face her mother...

CHAPTER SIX

'I'M NOT going back to Cladach to see Rick,' Helen Howard denied impatiently, annoyed at her mother's sniff of disapproval. 'I have to make permanent arrangements for the shop——'

'Of course you do.' Moira Howard didn't relent, and the dryness of her tone underlined her opposition. 'I would have thought the Frazers had caused this family enough trouble.'

'My relationship with Rick has no similarity whatsoever with Gran's and Malcolm Frazer's——'

'That's just what I mean. Your relationship is supposed to be non-existent and yet you defend it. Helen, that man used you to take the media pressure off him.' Picking up the stack of Sunday newspapers, she gestured at her daughter. 'I quote, "LOVESICK STARS AND SECRET LOVE-NEST." "STARS RUN AWAY TO HEAVEN——"'

'Enough!' Helen pleaded, green about the gills. The suspicion aired by her mother had also occurred to her as soon as she had cleared her head from the confusion of Rick's sudden and very public appearance.

'I suppose he is very good-looking,' her mother conceded as if he had a recognisable disease. 'He's probably been wooing gullible virgins since he's been in long trousers——'

'Mother!' Helen's tone hardened.

'All right. Bury your head in the sand if you want to. But don't say I didn't warn you.'

Helen was losing count of the people who had warned her about Rick Cameron. It had started with Peggy MacDonald, then Sarah Frazer, and since the recent exposé her mother, Terri Donovan and a host of other well-wishers had discreetly or not so discreetly fed her gossip about the film star. Even Michael Burton had snidely suggested that, if she couldn't cope with a light flirtation with him, he thought she was completely out of her depth with Cameron.

He was good-looking. She guiltily brought his face to mind, remembering the texture of his dark brown hair, matched with eyes that could look as hard and black as basalt but in the bright sunshine reminded her of the blend between wood bark and leaves with the blue sky above.

He hadn't even asked her if she was pregnant! The thought came back to her, breaking into her daydream. Perhaps he had pretended concern in an effort to keep her on the island. Her mind was tangled with suspicions and forbidden memories that would creep up on her just when she thought them vanquished. She needed fresh air, and, explaining briefly to her mother that she was going out, she decided to drive into the city and window-shop. As it was, the idea soon lost its appeal and she found her restless feet taking her to the parkland and eventually to the much worn path beside the Serpentine.

'You're marching again.' A voice very near to her ear made her jump, and she whirled around to find her per-secutor at her elbow, smiling at her as if the previous night had never happened.

'What are you doing here?' It seemed to be her lot in life to repeatedly ask Rick Cameron that very question.

'I work out in the park. I saw you way back, but I slowed down to a steady jog to let you burn off some of the fire.'

His story was plausible enough. He was wearing a navy sweat-shirt with a white stripe and logo across the chest, and matching tracksuit bottoms. The odour of male sweat was musky and not unpleasant, nor unfamiliar.

She tried to hide the sudden rush of awareness that flooded her body.

'I thought you'd be back on Cladach.' She kept walking, and he fell into step beside her, viewing her golden beauty with open admiration.

'I told you, I had some business to do. There are a few initial location shots in London and some publicity stuff to sort out.'

'Where is the bulk of the film being made? Somewhere exotic?' She was unwillingly curious.

'Edinburgh. That's why I decided to take the part. It's not really my sort of thing. I'm the hero in a mystery-suspense plot. I wanted to work in Scotland, so I compromised.'

'You'll have to drop the phoney accent,' she suggested tartly.

Rick gave a low growl of laughter. 'Ouch. Nothing about me is phoney, sweetheart. I grew up in the States. I visited Cladach for holidays.'

That surprised Helen. She had presumed he had gone to America, by whatever means, when he was sixteen.

'Why didn't you live with your family?' She frowned, baffled.

Rick shrugged, clearly regretting he had revealed so much. Stretching his arms above his head, he let them drop again, casting a calculating glance at the skies. 'It's going to rain soon. Do you want to come back to my place for lunch?'

'Why? Have you organised a cavalcade of Pressmen to record the occasion?'

'He-len...' he drew out her name in a slow drawl '...I want to talk to you. Meet me halfway...please.'

The appeal in his eyes was her undoing. Smart alec, the infuriating Rick Cameron, she could easily resist, but when his mood softened something similar happened to her insides. She melted and her mind took a holiday.

'I'd prefer a restaurant.' She tried to retrieve a modicum of control over the situation.

'Sure.' He gestured to his tracksuit. 'Mind if I change?'

'No, of course not.' She did, though. The idea of waiting patiently in the lounge of his apartment while he stripped naked and showered brought a rising sense of panic. She couldn't trust him an inch.

'I'll behave,' he promised, his eyes smiling knowingly into hers.

She cast him a non-comprehending glance, but she didn't think he was fooled for a minute. She supposed he must have intuitive powers to be such a good actor, but the thought didn't console her very much.

Helen found the mixture of lavender and cream tones in the apartment soothing. Rick moved over to the stereo and picked a Chris Rea album to play on compact disc. The sound quality was marvellous. Providing her with a glass of chilled white wine, he disappeared to have a shower.

While he was in the bathroom the phone rang, and Helen reluctantly answered it.

'Who are you?' a female voice demanded angrily. 'Is Rick there?'

'He's in the shower.' She could have bitten off her tongue. The smart click at the other end of the line suggested that the woman considered herself ill-used.

When he returned, dressed in a navy double-breasted suit, startlingly white shirt and maroon tie, and a silk handkerchief adorning his breast pocket, she forgot the call for a minute and swallowed. He looked totally different. Suddenly it was very easy to believe that he ran a production company.

'Who was on the phone?'

'I don't know. She hung up.' Her eyes were cool, lifting to meet his. 'If you get your picture in the papers kissing other women you must expect a certain amount of turbulence in your love-life.'

'Jealous?' he queried infuriatingly.

'Dreadfully.' She tried to equal his mockery.

'I know a good Italian restaurant. Do you like Italian food?'

He stood in front of the armchair she had chosen, legs slightly apart, his regard lazy and intimate, and it wasn't hard to guess what he was thinking.

'Italian will be fine.' Helen's eyes warned him that she wouldn't be pressurised into anything else.

A smile played around his mouth. 'OK,' he responded, and she wasn't sure whether he was agreeing to her unspoken terms or if he was just acknowledging her answer about the restaurant.

Helen received a further surprise when a cream BMW drew up as they left the apartment block and a uniformed chauffeur opened the door for them.

'Company car,' he acknowledged her dumbfounded expression. 'I thought you might feel safer.'

She felt uncomfortable as she remembered the angry words she had flung at him after the *Option Three* launch. That had been unforgivable, but she couldn't put the words together to apologise.

The restaurant was exclusive, and Helen felt distinctly under-dressed. Her white T-shirt and jeans made her look extremely youthful for her twenty-five years, and she wasn't wearing a scrap of make-up.

'You look fine.' Rick noticed the flutter of her hand to her hair, turning to acknowledge the waiter and ordering for both of them.

It was impossible not to notice the nudges and nods going around the restaurant. Helen was used to being noticed, but she was aware of an extra dimension to the curiosity when she was sitting across the table from Rick Cameron. He seemed impervious to it all, surprisingly so, considering the fact that some of the women in the restaurant were virtually eating him with their eyes. No wonder he was so colossally conceited.

'Ignore them.'

Helen was distracted from commenting on his ability to mind-read when she was presented with a glass of orange juice while he was being asked to sample the wine.

'I am over eighteen,' she pointed out stiltedly.

'You might be pregnant. In which case, you won't drink alcohol,' he returned in a matter-of-fact tone.

Helen didn't know how she restrained herself from up-ending the glass over his head. Whatever had possessed her to have lunch with him? She needed her head looking at.

'Which is why I think we should consider getting engaged.' He dropped the second bombshell in the same calm, seamless tone.

'No,' Helen responded in a low, driven voice, but it had the quality of protest rather than refusal.

'Being engaged would stop the Press hounding us,' he pointed out as if she hadn't spoken. 'And it would straighten things out on Cladach. They can be remarkably strait-laced about sex before marriage. We are lovers, Helen, however hard you try to pretend that morning in Castealcreag didn't happen.'

Scarlet-cheeked, Helen met his steady gaze with a hunted expression. 'We don't even like each other. How can we...?' She broke off, aware of the interest in their conversation and praying to God that no one could hear what they were saying.

'On the other hand, you could refuse... I can just see the headlines—"FALLEN VIRGIN BREAKS RUNAWAY STAR'S HEART." When I howl to the moon, Helen, no one gets any sleep.'

Regarding him with total disbelief, Helen was speechless. It was her worst nightmare come true, and he knew it.

'We're both sensitive about publicity,' she reminded him, desperately grasping at the straws of a defence.

'What have you got on me?' Leaning back in his chair, he observed her in a relaxed manner. 'Some half-baked story about a car crash. James exonerates me completely. If you leaked that story to the Press it would look spiteful and malicious. Not really in line with your image at all.'

'Dishing the dirt on your ex-lovers isn't your style either,' she pointed out frigidly.

Rick shrugged, his gaze lingering on the stiff lines of her mouth before studying the troubled expression in her eyes.

'There are ways, Helen. Crying into your beer in the wrong company usually does the trick.' With slow deliberation he took a jeweller's box out of his pocket and opened it. The light glittered over the diamonds surrounding the emerald heart of the ring. A hiss of excitement went around the restaurant and muffled orders were being given in the kitchen.

'Make your mind up. The champagne and gypsy violinist can't stay on ice indefinitely.'

'I hate you.' She spoke through gritted teeth.

He made a low growl in his throat. 'You're magnificent when you're angry. Now smile, or look fragile and overwhelmed. Baring your teeth at me is not in the best romantic tradition.'

Helen watched him nod to the waiter. The champagne corks popped and a ripple of applause went around the restaurant. The ring was taken between strong brown fingers and slid on Helen's reluctant hand, the happy couple locked in each other's gaze as the champagne frothed into glasses on every table. If their fellow diners had been near enough to see masculine triumph crowing over mutinous rebellion their rosy version of the event would have been severely challenged.

When the ordeal in the restaurant was over and she had been rather firmly persuaded to get into the waiting limousine she found not only had she to endure a mock engagement but further social engagements were expected of her.

'I've got to go to a dinner tonight. It's a social gathering of representatives from the various independent distilleries. I need a partner and it will look odd if I go with anyone else.'

'You could always go on your own,' she suggested coolly.

His eyes flicked over her, recognising the stubborn cast of her chin. 'But I don't want to go on my own, Helen. I want you to come with me.'

'Why should I? I don't know what you're up to or why this engagement is so important to you. All I know is that you don't give a thought to my feelings in all this!'

'Seven-thirty this evening.' He ignored her remonstrations. 'It's a formal affair, so dress accordingly.'

'You're unbelievable!'

'Now you're flattering me.' He turned the full power of his magnetic charm on her, his eyes holding that indecent heat that made her heart clamour and panic race through her body. The situation was tense; their eyes met, a growing awareness of need between them that was almost tangible on the air.

'Do you have to return to your single bed by twelve?' he queried, making her sound like some latter-day Cinderella.

'Stop it,' she whispered huskily, wishing desperately that there were some antidote for the weakness swamping her body.

The steamy look he gave her made her think of tropical rain forests, where everything was a mixture of mist and heat. His expression was potent with sensuality, his fingertips trailing the neckline of her T-shirt.

'It doesn't take long, does it?' He sounded hatefully amused. 'You can scream and shout as much as you like, but beneath all this Victorian propriety is a passionate woman who hasn't grown up enough to handle her own sexuality. I'm too old to bring you apples and carry your books home from school. Your eyes tell me you want me, then you make out that it's all my idea. Grow up, Helen, or I promise I'll make you.' Grasping her chin, he viewed the startled, hunted look she couldn't hide. 'And I'll enjoy doing it.' His mouth found Helen's in a potent demonstration of what he had in mind. Helen tried to twist away with a desperation born of fear. Shock waves thundered through her body. Her fingers skidded over the smooth fabric of his shirt, catching the side of his neck with her nails, then buried into his hair as her lips softened under the firm pressure of his mouth. His tongue slid along the wall of her teeth, the sensation making her gasp and vulnerable to further intimacy. She forgot about the car and the fact that there was a chauffeur separated from them by a wall of glass. Rick Cameron hadn't. His purpose was merely to staunch her rebellion and show her how futile any resistance was. He let his hand run lightly over her breast, down to her thigh, before easing back to view the moist shine of her lips. Helen's green misty eyes made him wish he hadn't got to spend the whole afternoon catching up with his company's commitments.

'The way you hate me is quite something.' Tracing her eyebrows and the fine line of her nose, he waited for her to regain control of her senses.

Disciplining her temper with difficulty, she wondered how she could ever lose herself enough to give him a foothold in her life. He was totally wrong for her. She wanted someone who was gentle, someone who cared. Rick Cameron mercilessly used her for his own purposes, callously manipulating her emotions until she felt like a puppet, with him holding all the strings.

Watching her changing expressions, her tormentor knew instinctively what she was thinking.

'What's the matter, Helen? Upset because you got the wrong Frazer? James would suit you,' he brooded sourly. 'You could both live in that polite never-never land where nothing nasty ever happens. You could play king and queen of Cladach, in your castle among the clouds. But something nasty would happen because I'd play Lancelot to James's Arthur—I couldn't help myself.'

Regarding him hostilely, she reflected that it wasn't the first time he had accused her of having designs on James Frazer.

'He's a gentleman,' she stated pointedly. 'It wouldn't occur to him to poach on his brother's territory.'

'Good. Then he'll stay away from you.'

Giving him a speaking look, Helen refused to be drawn into a debate on the issue of property rights. Rick had managed to put a ring on her finger and seduce her senses within the space of a few short hours. Her claims to independence had a hollow ring to them.

Helen chose a slinky black halter-neck for the dinner with the independent whisky distillers. Black stilettos and a mixture of pearls and gold for her jewellery created a vision of chic loveliness. She wore her hair up, fastened by a hidden comb.

Moira Howard viewed her with a worried look. 'If you hadn't met him in the park, do you think he would have bothered getting in touch?'

'Yes,' Helen replied with certainty. For whatever reason, Rick Cameron was not about to let her go.

'Why doesn't that sound very reassuring?' She frowned at her daughter. 'He doesn't make you happy. You're like a cat on hot bricks.'

Near, Helen thought. Despite her qualms about their relationship, she was dressed to kill. Her instincts were to fight back with every weapon in her armoury. Something told her that sex was a double-edged sword, and she wasn't the only one caught up in its dark enchantment.

'I don't recognise you in this mood.' Moira Howard felt her broad-mindedness shrink to a very real concern for her offspring. 'Will you be coming back?'

'Yes, of course.' She wished she was as sure as she sounded. She avoided Moira Howard's gaze. Helen didn't think her mother was in any doubt about the intimacy involved in her relationship with Rick Cameron. She supposed the news of her engagement would reassure the older woman, but she was reluctant to give credibility to the charade, despite the fact that her fiancé was determined to keep a high public profile.

'Helen——'

The door chimes saved Helen from some old-fashioned advice. Moira Howard purposefully made for the door.

Dressed in a dark evening suit, Rick was tall and impressive, his tanned skin in vivid contrast with the snowy-white linen shirt he wore.

'Mrs Howard.' He disarmed the avenging parent with a bouquet of flowers, and greeted Helen with a chaste kiss on the cheek. 'You look beautiful, darling.' His voice softened in supposedly stunned admiration.

Giving him a knowing look, she allowed him to arrange her wrap. She hoped he wouldn't pick up on her mother's failure to congratulate them. Awkward questions would be asked if he put her on the spot.

'The flowers are lovely, Mr Cameron...'

'Rick,' he interjected smoothly.

'Rick,' Moira Howard conceded. 'Helen said she might be late back. Have you any idea when these things finish?'

'It varies.' He was suitably vague. 'I'm sure Helen will find time to call you if she's going to be late.' Taking the younger woman's elbow, he urged her towards the door.

Helen was annoyed with her mother for interfering and irritated by the low laugh Rick Cameron emitted as soon as they were in his low-slung Porsche.

'What have you been telling her about me?' he queried, casting a glance over his shoulder as he released the hand brake and moved out into the street.

'I don't have to tell her anything. Isn't one Oscar enough? That was some performance.'

'Lust doesn't go down well with girls' mothers.' He sent her a mocking glance. 'Maybe I should have broached the subject of our engagement and really got into her good books.'

'Don't you dare!'

'You'll have to tell her soon. Why don't we break the happy news tonight? Or would you be disappointed if I got you home on time?'

It was a question Helen didn't want to contemplate. Something inside was wound up in a tight coil. She could protest as much as she liked about the way he conspired against her, but underlying the battle of words was a powerful attraction. It was something she ran from but never quite managed to escape. Rick Cameron pursued her relentlessly. She had wandered unwittingly into his private domain and he seemed intent on disarming the threat she embodied.

'I don't like living a lie. I haven't decided what I'm going to tell my mother yet.'

Rick glanced across at her. 'It won't be a lie if you're having a baby. My reasons for proposing the engagement aren't entirely selfish.'

'I'm touched.' She didn't bother to hide her disbelief. 'You'd better give me some background on this distillery business.' She was eager to change the subject. The fact that she couldn't deny that there might indeed be a reason for a hasty marriage was something else that troubled her. 'Tell me about malt whisky. What's so special about it, besides the price?'

'Philistine,' Rick accused her, sending her an appalled look. 'It's like comparing cheap fizzy white wine to vintage champagne.' For the rest of the journey he gave her a whistle-stop tour of the whisky business.

Malt whisky, it seemed, was far superior to grain whisky, being made out of malted barley rather than maize. It was made in hand-crafted copper 'pot' stills, rather than the industrial stainless steel used to make grain, and was added to give its poorer, almost tasteless cousin its flavour. Most of the well-known whiskies, he revealed, were blends with varying aged malts to give them their own distinctive character. The better-known malts such as Glenfiddich, Glenmorangie and Glenlivet had recently gained in popularity and were beginning to broaden their market.

'I managed to be in the right place at the right time when the upswing happened in the States. I merely tapped the nostalgia for the "auld country", and now Castealcreag is one of the best-selling malts in America. We're increasing our capacity to penetrate the British market but a good malt takes eight to twelve years to mature, so we have to plan ahead.'

'You seem very involved in the business.' Helen tried to put together a jigsaw with very few pieces. When Rick had arrived on Cladach she had received the impression that he had not been there for some time. James had visited him in Los Angeles when the crash had occurred, and Cathy Ferguson had revealed that this had been an attempt to heal the family rift. Yet his involvement with Castealcreag whisky appeared to stretch back years.

'Does that surprise you?' He turned into the car park of the Islay Hotel. 'I'm a major shareholder.'

'I thought James owned the distillery.'

Parking the car, he leant back in the seat to look at her.

'No, my father had enough sense to realise that James wasn't the least interested in business. He split the distillery between the three of us. I don't need Frazer money, in case that devious little mind of yours is weaving some kind of demonic plot out of the crash. All the revenue I receive is safely in the bank waiting for the go-ahead to build a hotel on Cladach and extend the distillery. I wouldn't spend a cent of my father's money on myself.'

'You sound very bitter,' Helen ventured, curious despite herself.

'Do I?'

Rick got out of the car, coming around to her side and courteously assisting her.

'It's all one-way traffic with us, isn't it?' she said bitterly. 'You made sure you discovered my reason for leaving London and taking up residence on the island. I ask you a question and you treat me like the cub reporter from the *Daily Globe*.'

Rick appeared to consider this and then shrugged. 'My father died five years ago.' He didn't look at her as he spoke, lifting his hand in greeting to someone in the distance. 'I returned to the island then, after fourteen years' absence. Looking back, I can see it was a bad time to introduce new ideas. James had just taken over the position of laird, and Sarah was as knee-jerk traditionalist as she is now. I was impatient for change and I suppose I tried to railroad them. Part of it was a juvenile attempt to get back at my father. We didn't get on,' he added unnecessarily.

'Why? James said you were both stubborn. Was it because you were too alike?'

Rick expelled his breath derisively. 'I suppose in the beginning I modelled myself on him. But then, he didn't recognise the influences in my life. He wanted me to be an islander and I wasn't. I chewed gum and played baseball. What was worse, I had all the other kids doing the same thing.'

Helen chuckled, imagining the heresy, but he didn't look amused. There wasn't time to delve any deeper. A tall kilted figure came over and shook Rick's hand.

'It's good to see you, Roderick. How's James? Is he walking yet?'

'Yes, he's doing well. Campbell Macallan, this is Helen Howard, my fiancée.'

The tall Scot congratulated him, turning to view Helen. 'Hmm, I recognise your face. The papers don't do you justice, my dear.'

Forcing herself to smile and accept the congratulations pressed upon her, she entered the foyer. The ballroom was set out with long tables, with a cleared area for the traditional dinner dance. Little flags with various tartan designs indicated who was sitting where. The table they joined was already partly occupied by Niall Ferguson, Cathy's father, and his wife Katy. Katy was from Leeds and had met her husband when he had been on business for the distillery in her home town. Niall Ferguson was the manager of the distillery, and he proudly accepted the export award when the ceremony began to applaud achievements of the independent distilleries.

'Are you enjoying yourself?' Katy Ferguson engaged her in conversation when the two men were absorbed with news from the other distilleries. 'Cathy sent her regards. She said the shop was all right and you weren't to worry. She'll stay on the island until James is all right. If she leaves she wants him strong enough to follow.'

Helen's eyes widened. 'Are they. . . ? I mean, I had no idea he was the man in her life.'

'Oh, yes. Cathy loves the island, you know, but she wants to see more of the world. Since the old laird died James has had little chance to do much more than keep everything on an even keel. She's like me—she doesn't understand why Rick, or Andy and Sarah if he's too busy, can't take over the day to day responsibilities of island life. Niall says it's being laird that does it, but this is the twentieth century and James isn't really interested in sheep farming.'

The plot thickened! James was like a man born to be king, going through the motions of the role assigned to him without any real fulfilment, while in the wings the two protagonists waited, one who wanted Cladach to enter the modern world, the other determined to keep the island firmly in the past.

'Have you fathomed all our secrets yet?' Rick murmured while they were dancing.

'I still don't know why you grew up in America.' She lifted her lashes just in time to see the shutters come down.

Forbidden territory, she acknowledged. Perhaps if she found out what he was so determined to protect she might be able to get free of him before...? Before what? Her mind closed off that avenue of thought: it was far too dangerous.

'When do you intend to return to the island?' Rick's voice close to her ear startled her.

Looking up into his tanned features, she picked up on his restlessness and wondered what had caused it. A muscle in his jaw tightened as if she angered him, and then she recalled his question, her fine brows drawing together. She felt as if she was drawing her mind back from a long way off.

'As soon as I can make arrangements. Work on the programme doesn't begin until October. Why?'

'I've left the helicopter at Glasgow airport. If you can be ready tomorrow I can book a flight from Heathrow and we can go together.'

On the face of it it was a practical solution. He had a way of making very bad ideas sound like common sense. She remembered the train journey.

'I don't want anyone following you to Cladach. A helicopter is hard to track.'

'Yes, all right,' she agreed wearily. She was already paying for imaginary sins; if she brought the full might

of the paparazzi to Cladach she shuddered to think what
he might do to her.

During the rest of the evening Rick was polite and
charming, and paradoxically felt miles away to Helen.
True, half his mind was absorbed by the intricacies of
the whisky trade. He was genuinely fascinated by the
subject, not that he drank overmuch. She supposed it
must be like producing good wine, more of an art form
than a weakness for alcohol. He was certainly knowledgeable and was consequently awarded a lot of respect
from representatives from the other distilleries.

'You're quiet,' he commented as he drove back towards Hampstead, the dark interior of the car intimate
after the glare and chatter of the dinner dance.

'It's been quite a day.' Helen stroked a tendril of hair
back behind her ear. Turning to look at him, she rested
her temple against the head-rest. 'You seemed to find
the proceedings fascinating.'

'I find it helps to have diversified interests. That way,
when life lets you down, the blow isn't so hard. Isn't
that what you're doing with the island shop? Or are you
thinking of getting rid of it?'

'No, I'm keeping the shop. You're right, it's nice to
have something away from the business. Do you intend
to spend more time on the island, now...?'

'Now my father's dead?' His mouth twisted cynically.
'Maybe. At the moment I haven't much choice in the
matter. James needs me.'

Drawing up beside the house, he accompanied her to
the door. The small porch light gave his skin a sallow
look, his hair and eyebrows almost black. Glancing at
his watch, he gave her a meaningful look.

'Cinderella would be in rags by now. I should be able
to get you on to my flight tomorrow, so be ready for
about ten o'clock.'

Bending his head, Rick brushed her lips lightly with
his, drawn back by the soft quiver of her mouth, his

hands sliding down her back, appreciating the naked length of golden skin and the fine arch of her spine.

'I'll see you tomorrow.' His voice sounded like rough velvet.

'Goodnight.' What was happening to her, meekly bidding him farewell, not even attempting to protest at the kiss? What was worse, she suspected it wasn't the liberty-taking that bothered her.

She watched him go to his car, feeling the adrenalin drain away as the Porsche disappeared down the road. A desperate restlessness swept over her and she couldn't hide how she felt when her mother opened the door.

'I thought you'd lost your key.' The well-rehearsed excuse was executed smoothly, but Moira Howard missed nothing. 'You're still going to the island, then?' It was said as a foregone conclusion.

'Yes.' Helen followed her mother into the house, taking the brandy that was offered without demur.

'Don't rush into anything, Helen. I know mothers are supposed to lean heavily towards commitment, but the way you feel... well, it might burn itself out.'

A shadow crossed Helen's fine features and she shivered. 'I think it's a bit late for that, Mother.' She placed the smooth glass against her cheek, trying to cool her blood. 'Rick and I... we became engaged this afternoon.'

CHAPTER SEVEN

'WHAT would you like to see?' Rick spoke over the sound of the helicopter's blades beating the air. 'We can either take the most direct route or follow the West Highland Way.'

'That would be nice.' Helen indicated her preference for the latter. She had never covered the route by car, flying for most of the journey on her first visit and using the train on the memorable return to the island. The helicopter gave an excellent compromise between the arduous but scenic road route and the speed of travelling by air.

'The footpath starts at Milngavie on the edge of Glasgow. It follows a lot of ancient roads, some Highland paths, others military roads built in the eighteenth century to quell the Jacobite clansmen.'

'Have you ever walked it?' she asked innocently.

'Not all of it.' A degree of self-mockery coloured his tone. 'That's what exiles do—prowl around the boundaries of their old home. Didn't your grandmother ever visit Scotland?'

'I think she visited Edinburgh once or twice. And she had friends on Islay. She never went back to Cladach, though. Aunt Fi asked us to visit many times, but...' She shrugged, wishing she hadn't accepted her mother's plausible excuses quite so readily.

'Small communities can be a strength, but they can also impose harsh discipline on nonconformists. I can understand how she felt.'

Helen glanced at him curiously. The more she found about him, the more he puzzled her. She had always supposed his 'exile', as he called it, had been voluntary. The bitterness in his tone suggested otherwise. What sort of father, however wayward his son, would have made him homeless at sixteen? She wondered if he had followed in his grandfather's tradition and got a little too friendly with one of the island girls. That sort of complication wouldn't surprise her at all!

Helen regarded him covertly while he competently handled the controls. He wore a collarless turquoise T-shirt with white shorts, his long brown legs bare and well-muscled. He was incredibly talented, she mused. He ran his own production company, was at the top of his profession as an actor, could hold his own with executives from the whisky trade, and was no mean pilot to boot. With such mental accolades he could consider himself blessed, which was why it seemed almost too good to be true that he was endowed with such physical attractiveness. Helen's fingers curled into the seat to subdue the impulse to stroke the hard masculine thigh so close to her own. She could feel his body heat, and her own skin became sensitised in turn. Sweeping her hair back from her neck, she let the air cool her nape, her green eyes provocatively sensual when he glanced at her, pointing out Loch Lomond below them.

'The loch used to see many a battle between farmers at the foot of the loch and cattle traders to the north.' He continued to act as tourist guide, but his eyes flicked from her breasts to her lips and then met hers with a lethal glint of amusement that suggested he knew exactly what she was thinking. 'Beautiful, isn't it?'

'Yes.' She looked away, staring down into the expanse of water as they followed the length of the loch northwards. Hills rose up all around them as they flew over the islands of the loch. White, spumy clouds frothed against a blue sky, catching the light from the sun and becoming edged in gold. Everything seemed to call to Helen's senses.

'Shall we run the gauntlet of public curiosity in a hotel or pub, or would you prefer to buy a picnic and take a break on Rannoch Moor?'

It was such a lovely day that the thought of being inside was abhorrent, especially so with their current level of exposure in the media. Helen had little desire to repeat the public charade surrounding their engagement. She was rather surprised that Rick hadn't involved her in a Press conference; after all, the engagement was supposed to put an end to Press speculation. The episode in the restaurant had merely increased their fervour.

'We'll have a picnic, shall we?'

Rick nodded, frowning as he thought about where he could land near the required shop.

'Crianlarich's about the best bet,' he informed her. 'There's nothing much in the way of towns between here and Fort William.'

They followed the lochshore from Rowardennan to the head of Loch Lomond, passing over woodland flanking Ben Lomond and making out walkers here and there scrambling over the sometimes rough terrain.

'We're coming into MacGregor country; Rob Roy's cave is north of Inversnaid.'

Rob Roy, so named because of his days as a cattle thief and his red hair, had been a cattle drover come upon hard times due to the absconsion of his head drover with all the cash for the spring sale of cattle. The Duke of Montrose had been the main creditor and had burnt down Rob Roy's house, evicting his family, which had earned him the MacGregor as an enemy and long-term reiver on his estate.

Despite his claim to be more of the States than Scotland, Rick Cameron had much of the barbaric Scot in his own nature. It didn't take a lot of imagination to see him as a cattle raider, becoming involved in bitter and bloody feuds.

Helen did the shopping, providing them with a substantial picnic. Crianlarich sported a store and a post office but was quite small. After passing the lowland belt of commerce and industry, it was amazing to see just how empty Scotland was.

Their journey continued, pushing deeper into the north-west. Their goal, Rannoch Moor, was one of the largest moors in Britain. It was a giant grave for the massive forest that had once populated the land, now showing its smiling summer face of purple heather, waving bracken, bleached grass and trickling burns.

Rick landed the helicopter beside one of the burns, where great grey slabs of stone provided a picnic table. He clearly had some knowledge of the moor as he'd chosen a relatively dry spot in among a complex array of upland peat bogs. In the distance she could see the bright green patches of sphagnum moss and the fluffy heads of cotton grass.

Rick spread out a picnic blanket before straightening and looking around him at the wilderness of Rannoch Moor with its distant surrounding bastion of the Grampian mountains.

'It's evil in the winter,' he informed her, the blue sky above and the hot sunshine giving the moor a benign, slumbering appearance.

Helen could believe it. She was also very conscious of being completely alone with Rick, and along with that came the perception that he meant it to be that way. It had been her choice, she realised. She could have insisted on a hotel for lunch. There was a scarcity of towns and villages, but lone hotels populated the Highlands, there for the shooting and fishing parties that came rain or shine.

'You seem to like places that are wild and free; why do you want to change Cladach?' she asked, trying to quell a bubble of panic rising inside her. Her voice sounded strange, thick and husky, and Rick viewed her with an answering male awareness that made her blood trickle hotly through her veins.

'Scotland was once heavily populated; so were the islands. You've read the story of St Kilda. When the people left, they lost something. But it was a harsh, unrelenting life. I want to strike a balance the islanders can live with. We've got the distillery, the sheep and the island itself. A hotel would bring in some life for the young people. This is nice for jaded city folk like you and me, but if you grow up with it it's as familiar as red brick and factories in an industrial town.' He sighed. 'Don't be fooled by James and Sarah. They both went away to university; they've both travelled. There are very few financial restrictions on the way they want to live, and they have a healthy supply of guests to keep them amused.'

She frowned, impressed by his fervour but unsure of his motives. 'You said your plans for change were a juvenile attempt to get back at your father. Is that still true?'

'I don't know.' He was honest enough to have doubts. As he sat on one of the grey rocks his brows drew together in a dark frown. 'Maybe I'm just doing it for myself. Cladach feels like home, despite the past. Los Angeles is OK, but it's the exact opposite, always changing...rootless. I need a bit of both. I want to live on Cladach when I'm not filming, and I want something to do when I'm there. I've talked to the islanders.' He sent her a defensive glance. 'What they'd like is something that takes advantage of the island's beauty but doesn't destroy it. I'm not planning to build Caesar's Palace.' Exasperation tinged his voice. 'Just a good-quality hotel with sports facilities.'

'And they want it?'

'Yes, they want it.' He sounded irritated by her assumption that he would press ahead if they didn't. 'They want their children to stay. They want to watch their grandchildren grow up, not become strangers who visit from Glasgow or Inverness three times a year.'

'It sounds like a good idea,' she soothed him, and he smiled and looked down for a moment, his eyes keen as they met hers.

'Not only Sally can beat the drum, you know. We're quite alike in some ways. Besides not liking baseball, my father didn't think much of girls either. That's why she tried so hard to adopt his every thought. It was a rather futile attempt to gain his approval.'

Helen watched the dark memories seize him again and felt an unwilling sympathy. 'He sounds like a hard man.'

'Yes,' he agreed without further clarification, 'he was.'

The man was the emotional equivalent of Fort Knox, Helen thought frustratedly. Imagining she could ever get him to divulge those secrets he was so protective of was pie in the sky.

'What makes you so scared of men, Helen?' He surprised her with the question, meeting the startled uplift of her lashes with a determination she was all too familiar with.

'What makes you think I'm scared?' She felt her bravado shrivel when faced with the power of his gaze.

'Because you're on the run.' He approached her slowly, easing himself down on to his knees beside her. 'It's not making love; you want that, it's there in your eyes. I know you're sensitive to the Press intruding after the Gary Chambers incident, but that didn't really say much except that you had the good sense not to get too involved with a lowlife like him.'

'They made me sound like a freak...' she burst out emotionally. 'I suppose, if you ever get to tell tales about me, it will correct that impression.' She tried to move back but he grabbed her arm.

'I'm not doing any of this for fun, Helen.' He caught her other wrist as she pushed against his chest and brought her close to him. Her ear was pressed against his chest, picking up the steady beat of his heart, her hair like spun gold gathering up against his T-shirt.

'Really?' Tossing her head back, she looked up at him, her expression resentful. 'You're not averse to taking some pleasure from our mythical relationship, are you, Rick?'

'I see nothing mythical about it.' He viewed the tender curve of her mouth contradicted by eyes that were valiantly sending out battle signals as if she had to convince herself of the need for war. 'Once tasted, your kind of fire is addictive. I want more, Helen. You were making some powerful promises in the car yesterday and I think it's about time you kept them. Otherwise I might think you're a tease——'

'I'd rather drown in a peat bog.'

'I don't think you would, but...' Moving swiftly, Rick Cameron lifted her into his arms and went to the edge of the stone slabs that overlooked a stretch of thinly reeded water.

'Don't you dare!' she threatened impotently, her hands tightening on his shoulders.

'I think you should know by now that I dare.' Rick smiled evilly at her, rocking on his feet in a manner that suggested they might both get a soaking. Remembering the episode at Roin Bagh, Helen was in little doubt that he was willing to get her thoroughly wet. Linking her arms around his neck, she was determined to take him with her. Their eyes met in fiery conflagration.

He was too close! She was holding him for protection but it was a lover's embrace. His eyes darkened, his gaze locking hers in a world of erotic intimacy.

'This place keeps its secrets, Helen. Whatever happens here will never find its way to the Press... to anyone.'

How could he make her feel this way? Helen shivered despite the heat. He was an arch manipulator: he had forced her to wear his ring; he had ignored all laws of

hospitality and entered her bedroom at Castealcreag
and...

She shuddered when he kissed her, her lips taken and
moulded to the shape of his, her soft moan sounding
suspiciously like pleasure. It must have been the sort of
buzz gamblers experienced when they placed a bet with
money they didn't have. A dark thrill which they knew
to be utterly senseless but could not resist.

He allowed her little time to think, his mouth returning to hers as soon as he had lowered her to her feet.
Her fingers loosened on his shoulders, entwining in his
hair, her breasts pressed against the hard wall of his chest,
his hands on her waist, almost spanning it, tightening
to feel the fragile beauty of her body so exquisitely
delicate against his male strength.

Easing back, Rick viewed her with intimate warmth;
her green eyes were wary but softly lit with embers of
sensual need.

'So what makes you fight so hard?' He tugged the
lace bow free on her bodice, one finger tugging the fragile
fastening so that it unravelled, falling open.

Swallowing drily, Helen scanned his features as if she
was trying to understand what it was about him that
made her behave in such a wanton fashion. Heated
colour lay across her cheekbones as she felt the intrusive
finger lightly insert itself under the slack cotton and discover the hard peak of her nipple.

'I seem to have very bad taste in men.' She forced the
words from her lips as he exposed the globe of her breast,
watching it nestle in his hand with obvious satisfaction.

'Chambers and Burton were definitely mistakes, but
you're improving.' His thumb stroked against her,
causing the pink satin peak to stiffen with blatant
invitation.

Helen saw the intent in his eyes and felt panic flood
her body. Her restless movement was stilled as his mouth
fastened on her breast, and she felt her protest drift into

the edge of consciousness as her senses became start-lingly alive and begged for satiation.

Seconds later his mouth consumed hers and Helen was kissed into shivering acquiescence, aware of his hand pushing her skirt up her thigh and feeling the sun's heat compete with his touch as it caressed the naked flesh.

When he lowered her on to the grass every part of her was burning. She arched her body up against the hard male frame above her, aware of his tantalising brown skin separated from her flesh by the turquoise T-shirt he wore. Grasping the edge, she pushed it up his back, feeling the lithe, straining muscles of his body as he thrust his hips against hers to let her feel the arousal of his body and to ease and inflame the growing ache in her loins.

Helen felt bereft when he pulled back from her, lying back on the ground with a sulky, sensual pout, her eyes consuming him as he pulled off his T-shirt. He was ar-rogantly sure of his own sexuality, she reflected, knowing he was aware of her appreciative gaze. His muscles rippled with quiet efficiency as he stripped the skirt from around her legs. The white triangle of silk guarding her loins was summarily dismissed, but not before he had traced the barrier across her stomach and the top of her thighs. Helen broke free of the savage torment of his eyes, turning her face away, biting into the base of her thumb. She wouldn't beg him to touch her, to put an end to such torment, and she knew he intended to torment her as much as his own body reactions would allow. She felt the removal of her last garment, felt him run his hands lightly over her legs, gripping her knees and exerting pressure to expose her sensitive inner thighs to his caress. He promised but he didn't give. The soft brush of his lips moved on to her stomach, light kisses circling the taut peaks of her nipples until she almost shrieked with exasperation.

'What's the matter, sweetheart? What is it that you want?' His voice tormented her, his fingers brushing her hair back from her face.

His teasing was intolerable. Throwing caution to the winds, she reached up to pull his dark head down to hers, kissing him with a fervour that destroyed any myth that she wasn't fully acquiescent to their lovemaking. Her hands developed a growing skill in arousing him, directed by his groans and shudders of pleasure. This in turn distracted Rick from any other intention but satisfying their mutual need, and she wrapped herself around him in primeval coupling, her golden limbs inviting him into the captivity of her body, deeper and deeper until he was lost to any other demand than to be part of her.

The sun was considerably lower in the sky before sanity returned, and Helen pulled away from Rick, who appeared to have gone to sleep, and dressed herself with considerable agitation. What on earth was she doing, behaving so wantonly with a man who was her...what? Enemy? Her breasts reacted sensitively to the renewed confinement; her whole body felt languorous and continued to play traitor to her mind. It wasn't as if it had just been once! She had spent virtually the whole afternoon under the seductive spell Rick wove over her senses.

Going to the edge of the stone slabs, she looked over the vast moor. She knew from the gossip of friends and colleagues that most of them would leap at the chance of finding a lover like Rick Cameron, but it didn't feel right for her and the possibility of becoming emotionally entangled with him scared her half to death. It had taken her mother twelve years to even begin to consider a romantic attachment after John Howard had died. She knew if she allowed herself to believe herself in love with Rick she would leave herself open to pain and betrayal.

'Don't tell me you still think the peat bog was preferable?' Rick linked his arms around her from behind, nuzzling her neck. 'Are you trying to resurrect all that maidenly modesty?'

'Are you?' she responded coolly. 'I suppose you'd prefer me to be angry—it stops me asking anything from you, doesn't it?'

'Like what?' He turned her round, viewing her with curiosity.

'Like the reason why we're creating this elaborate smokescreen for the Press.'

A humourless smile curled his mouth. 'Persistent, aren't you?'

'So you still think I'd betray you?' Her green eyes glittered with challenge.

'What? You mean after giving up your body so delightfully? It doesn't change a thing.' He turned away to pick up his T-shirt, meeting her eyes as he pulled it down over his chest. 'Don't look so wounded, angel; there are a lot of things I would do for you.'

Giving his amused smirk a contemptuous blast, she turned away. 'I'm cold. I want to go!' Rubbing her arms, she tried to ease the chill running over her skin.

Silently they made their way to where the helicopter stood, a bizarre incursion into the natural landscape. It was warmer inside, the glass bubble heated up by the strength of the sun, untouched by the moor breeze.

'So...' she fiddled with her ring when they were seated and strapped in, watching it gleam in the evening light '...how long is this fictitious engagement going to last?'

'As long as it takes.'

'For what?'

Pushing a hand through his dark, unruly hair, he gave a careless shrug. 'To find out whether you're pregnant or not and for the Press to lose interest in us.'

Closing the discussion, he started the rotor blades whirring above them and concentrated on manoeuvring the helicopter into the air.

The sky was a mass of red, amber and gold. Helen looked around her, feeling like a bird soaring above the land as they skimmed the moorland and headed westwards towards Fort William. The remaining journey was passed in silence except for Rick pointing out landmarks. The Long Island chain stretched out like a sea-dwelling primeval monster making its way to the west. Cladach was tiny, but expanded rapidly on approach, the mass of sea-birds making Rick cautious as they settled down inland at Samhrad Taigh.

'Home, sweet home.' He regarded her tolerantly as she viewed the cottage with love. 'Don't get too fond of chintz and home-made lampshades. Somehow I can't see you in a spinster's cottage knitting socks for fishermen.'

Helen gritted her teeth. No one could annoy her more than Rick Cameron. 'How do you see me?' she asked sweetly, to see his mouth curl up into a grin.

'I'll tell you tonight.'

'I beg your pardon?' She viewed him with alarm, only to see his gaze go past her.

'You have company.'

Momentarily distracted, she waved to Cathy, who had opened the cottage door. 'From now on I insist we keep our relationship strictly business,' she stipulated to deaf ears.

Rick unstrapped himself and climbed out, coming round to help her. 'I'll be back later,' he said close to her ear before Cathy was near enough to overhear what was being said.

'Tha la math ann. Ciamar a tha thu?' Cathy greeted them in Gaelic.

'Never better,' Rick responded to her greeting. 'I've convinced Helen to marry me.'

He really was a terrific actor, Helen had to admit. The affectionate warmth he turned on for their spectator almost had her convinced. Lurking suspicions that the fictitious engagement was becoming more realistic by the

second added to the inner turmoil caused by her relin-
quishing of sanity on Rannoch Moor.

'Congratulations.' Cathy smiled warmly, glancing
curiously at Helen, whose expression held more than a
tinge of resentment.

Quickly hiding her feelings, Helen smiled. She found
it disturbing how easily people accepted their involvement. Even Moira Howard had regarded her
daughter's engagement with a gloomy inevitability.
Despite her mother's infatuation with show business, she
had a jaundiced view of the relationships it spawned.

When Rick went Helen was glad to share a pot of tea
with Cathy Ferguson, sinking back among the chintz and
admiring the pale pink and white roses adorning a glazed
jug that decorated one of the bamboo tables.

'Quite a whirlwind romance,' Cathy teased her.
'You've obviously stopped fighting.'

'Not really.' Helen found the subject of her relationship with Rick demanded artifice on her part as
well as his. 'In fact, the fights are probably worse, and
far more frequent.' She smiled to take away the damning
truth of her statement.

'Och, I can see you'd fight, the pair of you. You're
both stubborn. You look a lot more relaxed than you
did, though. When you first came to Cladach you looked
haunted. It's good to see things turn out right.'

'What about you?' Helen was grateful to change the
subject. She realised that Cathy had her own family and
friends, but also knew they were not always the easiest
people to talk to. When the problem was James Frazer,
the laird of Cladach, the situation complicated itself. The
islanders would expect the laird to fulfil his responsibilities, and Cathy might well seem disloyal, expecting
him to consider her first.

'My mother said she'd spoken to you. She said you
didn't realise I was involved with James. That's not too
surprising; I haven't been a regular visitor to Castealcreag

recently.' Cathy's small urchin face took on lines of
sadness. 'James says I should get the travel bug out of
my blood. He says he can't leave the island, that it's his
duty to stay.' She wrinkled her nose in disgust. 'He says
he'll wait for me, but I don't want to go without him
and I can hardly force the issue at the moment, not with
things the way they are, James still convalescing and
Sarah with the new baby.'

Cathy clearly felt under similar obligation to Rick.
Everyone on the island seemed tied up in an ancient tapestry that demanded loyalty and sacrifice. Maybe it was
natural to them, taken in with their mother's milk, but
for her it was bewildering. Which begged questions about
her inability to get out of the web of blackmail and de-
ception Rick had woven around her.

When Cathy had left for the evening Helen rehearsed
her confrontation with Rick. She was going to restate
her terms. The situation would get impossible if they
continued with their affair. She was getting too used to
his presence in her life. Her tendency to fall in with his
plans was positively half-witted and suggested subcon-
scious yearnings that she didn't dare think about.

Rick hadn't turned up by eleven, and she stifled a
yawn, deciding to go to bed. He must have got involved
with business matters, she decided, and if it was anything to do with the distillery it would cancel her from
his thoughts.

Cathy had thoughtfully made the bed with the clean
linen airing in the heated cupboard. Peach-coloured
sheets and pillow slip were covered with a candlewick in
the same colour. Candlewick suited the cottage, and
Helen had forgone the usual duvet despite the latter's
convenience.

When Rick Cameron let himself into the cottage he
stood by the side of the bed, watching her while she slept.
She was restless, her honey-coloured hair tangled silkily
around her. Her lashes were darker than her hair and

fanned her cheeks, flickering now and then as she dreamt. White-hot sparks fired his blood, his thoughts drawn away from the various concerns in his life to the sole object of possessing the slim form moving restlessly against the covers.

Kicking off the bedclothes, she exposed her lemon silk nightshirt, her knee raised rubbing the sheet, revealing the tight curve of her buttock to his drugged gaze. Pulling at the studs on his denim shirt, he freed his skin to the coolness of the night air. She made him feel powerful and virile in a way he had never experienced before. He had a number of affairs behind him that had brought him varying degrees of physical satisfaction but never this arousal of the senses that heightened every touch, every contact. Sliding his jeans from his skin, he remembered her touch, the mixture of innocent sexuality and guilt that would torment her and make her fret until he took her deeper into the realms of sensuality and set her free. Daggers of passion forked into his loins, making him seek her warmth, rub his face against the softness of her hair, his hands tracing her warm curves under the silk nightshirt she wore.

'Rick,' she mumbled, her mind still clouded with dreams. She shivered as he opened the buttons on her nightshirt, and she frowned slightly, her eyes shooting open at the demanding pressure of his hips, naked against her exposed skin.

'You're very sexy when you sleep.' Rick covered her sleep-slackened lips, his tongue probing her teeth while his body continued to move arousingly against hers. 'Were you dreaming of me?' he asked her minutes later, viewing the swollen pink lines of her mouth with satisfaction.

'No!' she denied, trying to summon up indignation.

Laughing softly, he nibbled at her ear, and Helen shivered when his tongue explored the delicate inner crevices.

'Liar.' He pushed the lapel of her nightshirt back, his hand clenched in the lemon silk as his mouth moved moistly over her upper chest, seeking and finding the darkened nipple that peaked as his lips shaped it and his teeth nibbled at the sensitive tip.

'Oh.' The soft, aching sound that left Helen's lips was telling enough. She put her hands up to her face, and then her fingers ran into her hair, leaving her face uncovered to be kissed. Her forehead, eyes, heated cheeks were caressed as his hands worked wicked magic on her body.

'I'm halfway to paradise,' he drawled with laconic sexuality that acknowledged the way her hips were moulding to his, accepting the masculine demand being increasingly imposed upon the delicate portal of her body.

'What are you doing here?' She tried to wriggle away from him, but his body weight kept her flat against the mattress.

'Work it out.' He took her mouth with flagrant disregard for her fledgeling protest, the intensity of his kisses suggesting that her twelfth-hour bid to turf him out of her bed was not being taken seriously.

'Rick, we've got to talk...' Her words were barely audible, and the path of kisses burning down her throat made her lose the sense of what she was trying to say.

'Talk to me all you like, baby,' he muttered huskily, intrigued by the sight of his hand against the pale gold of her stomach. 'I'm listening.'

The sheer mockery almost broke through but was translated into sexual combat, Rick breathing in swiftly when her nails scraped over his rib-cage, one flattening over the muscled length of his thigh, the other moving stealthily down his stomach and drying up his breath in his throat.

'God, I'm beginning to need this.' His voice was husky and deep, his eyes dark and passionate as they met

Helen's green lambent gaze. He watched her eyes close and her lips part as the probing heat of his body surged into hers.

Minutes later Helen was sliding her hands feverishly over his sweat-slicked body with the wonder of an artist fashioning a new creation. His shoulders felt like molten steel, the hard bone and straining muscles moving in symmetry with the thrusting movements of his hips. The line of hair marking his breastbone was wet and fanned out against his brown skin, his face a rigid mask of desire. Fire moved like a flashing sword within her, the duel too brilliant to follow. He rose above her, his shadow cast into giant form against the ceiling by the subdued bedside lamp. Yet he poured his strength into her body, the whole endeavour of his male power to follow the explosive path of passion and find its zenith in her arms.

'Stop running from me, Helen,' he breathed into her mouth as the last quake of passion ebbed between them. Closing his eyes, Rick felt the heavy tide of sleep flood around him. 'Because if you don't,' his voice was almost a whisper, 'I'll make your life hell.'

The woman beside him failed to respond and his eyes opened to see the heavy cast of her features; then he allowed himself the luxury of her warmth as he wrapped himself around her and fell into a deep, exhausted sleep.

CHAPTER EIGHT

HELEN awoke alone the next morning, her feelings about Rick's midnight raid mixed. She had intended to make some rules to the dangerous game they were playing but instead he had broken into her sleep, taken advantage of her vulnerable state and had dazed her with the urgency of his passion until she had thought of nothing else but appeasing it. Her body, however, felt languid and womanly in a way that brought an unbidden smile to her lips. Some subterranean knowledge told her that she was more alive than she had ever been, and to have the promise of her sexuality met and completed was a satisfaction no other could match.

She heard the helicopter when she was having breakfast and, by the proximity of the sound, she guessed it had landed near by. This time he knocked on the cottage door, and she realised why when she saw Cathy Ferguson pulling up in her car.

'Pay no mind to me—I'm just here to unpack some of the supplies that came with Murdo yesterday,' she informed them, her eyes twinkling.

'I'll bring you a cup of tea,' Helen promised, glancing up into Rick's appreciative gaze and giving him a look of reproof in return.

'And what have I done?' he requested, unabashed, sitting down at the breakfast table and pinching a slice of toast.

He was easy with it all, she reflected. He demanded none of the order she had previously demanded of life. He wasn't the least bit cautious, and he made her feel like one of those perilous surfers at the top of a wave.

Raising a dark eyebrow, Rick waited. He was casual but smartly dressed that morning, stone-coloured trousers matched with a beige sweater with a crew neck and cable design. Seeing that she was absorbed with him and had temporarily lost the thread of her thought, he crunched the toast between white teeth and indulged in a similar appraisal of her finer points.

'Have you got a key to my cottage?' The incensed look came back again and he could tell she was angry with herself.

'There's one at Castealcreag. The cottage was once part of the estate; Fiona MacSween never bothered to change the locks.'

'How very convenient.' She poured the tea out for Cathy, not enjoying the thought that she had become some sort of feudal privilege for the lairds of Castealcreag.

'Not really. I don't think Fiona was ever in danger from any of the Frazer men.' His eyes laughed at her, the intimate knowledge in their depths making her blush.

'She clearly demanded a level of respect,' she pointed out stiffly. 'I'd rather you waited until you were invited before you come into my home.'

'Why?' He waited with infuriating interest for her to back up her request.

'Because I prefer it that way.' She had no intention of taking the argument on to his territory. Giving him a prim, missish look, she picked up the cup and saucer and took it to Cathy in the shop.

Cathy thanked her, glancing up from the box she was opening and doing a double-take at her friend's perplexed expression.

'Don't tax yourself—they're not worth it.'

Helen smiled weakly. 'I'll be through to help you shortly. Shout if you want anything.'

Rick watched her reappear, a knowing look on his face that did nothing to soothe her. 'It will get easier, honey. You don't give yourself very much time.' Rising, he came across to where she stood near the door. 'I'm going to Inverness to pick up Sarah and Andy.' Enfolding her in his arms, he felt the rigidity of her body and acknowledged the passive resistance expressed eloquently by her beautiful eyes. 'James suggested you come to Castealcreag tonight to welcome Sarah and the baby home. And to celebrate our engagement, of course.' He saw the doubt in her expression and smiled. 'Sad about not making lady of the manor? Don't worry, I'm far wealthier than James. If you want an island I'll buy you one.'

'Very funny.' Helen succeeded in pulling away. She was tempted to flirt with James, since it so obviously got under his skin. If Cathy hadn't been her friend she wouldn't have been able to resist.

'What time?' she queried with a distinct lack of grace.

'I'll pick you up around seven-thirty.' His eyes melted her, and for a second that lasted an eternity she found it very hard to remember why she was annoyed with him. It didn't take her long to remember. 'I'll arrange for you to have a room if you want to stay over.' He laughed, holding up his hands in mock defence when she aimed a slap at his head. 'You'll change your mind and have to share my bed. I'd much rather sneak into yours.'

'I have every intention of coming back to Samhrad Taigh, and I want the key to the cottage—is that understood?' Her fingers itched to hurl something at him, and he noticed the expression in her eyes and retreated.

'You need a good night's sleep,' he advised with overdone solicitude, moving out into the shop and looking hard done by for Cathy Ferguson's benefit. 'She won't even kiss me.' The roguish gleam in his eye made the other girl give him an impatient look.

'I'm sure you don't deserve to be kissed. Away with you, and let us get on with our work.'

Helen joined Cathy in the shop when Rick had departed, pleased to see that the new stock she had ordered had arrived and the variety available had improved. She had managed to extend the reading material too, from a few traditional and old-fashioned magazines to a modern selection. There were even a couple of comics, which had been requested by the children.

'I hope they're translated into Gaelic, or Sarah will have your skin.'

Helen shrugged. 'Little Campbell suggested them. They already watch the cartoons, so it's rather futile to deprive them of what they want.'

'Hmm. The tables and chairs arrived for outside the shop. That's another fight you'll have on your hands: Sarah likes to make tourists feel as uncomfortable as possible so that they leave quickly.'

'Well, I'm not Sarah,' she evinced with laudable conviction. She supposed at heart she had already cast her lot in with Rick. Cladach had to be a viable community to survive, not a fossil from the past. Perhaps she was in the mould of Clara MacSween—she had broken rules too! 'I was going to introduce the idea as a facility for weary islanders to have refreshments. Some of my customers just come here to chat; now they can have a cup of coffee at the same time.'

'Are you going to charge?' There was an imp of mischief in Cathy's eyes.

'No.' Helen read her expression and understood it. Hospitality was the island way. To charge for refreshments would be outright heresy. 'It's the thin edge of the wedge. Once the practice is established, I don't see why we shouldn't extend the facility to tourists at a reasonable cost.'

'Very diplomatic,' Cathy chuckled. 'I hope some of it rubs off on Rick. He could have had the hotel built by now if he weren't so bull-headed. He doesn't suffer fools lightly. In that, he's just like his father.'

Helen depressed her mouth comically. 'Don't tell him that. He takes great pains to be different.'

'Well, he would,' Cathy agreed solemnly.

For a moment Helen thought she was going to break through the wall of silence that surrounded Rick's past, but the other woman lost interest in the subject and she was unable to ask questions without revealing her lack of knowledge about Rick's background.

Helen heard the helicopter return around midday, so presumably Sarah would be able to rest before the evening's celebrations. Remembering her last brush with Sarah Frazer, she viewed the evening ahead with trepidation. She was not one, however, to score points. Eschewing one of her more figure-hugging, exotic dresses, she chose instead an olive-green culotte-skirt with matching waistcoat, wearing a cream blouse underneath. Knowing that Sarah's figure would take some time to recover, she did not want to spark off any further animosity by trying to attract attention to her own slender lines.

Rick, when he arrived, looked unusually formal. He wore a double-breasted suit in a black check, with a white shirt and a crimson tie with muted Paisley pattern on it. His dark hair was brushed back and, although not as severely gelled as it had been during the ceilidh, he had obviously used something to train it into respectable order.

'It's been hours,' he murmured in parody of a man deeply in love, and Helen ignored him and the tease in his eyes, turning to the mirror to fix one of her Mexican-style earrings.

'How's Sarah?'

'Unusually polite.' He watched the small feminine adjustments she made with interest. 'The baby's a sweetheart. It stopped crying as soon as we got into the helicopter.'

'That will be a godsend if she starts crying at four in the morning.' Helen was droll.

'Could be very inconvenient,' he considered the idea. 'There's another little girl I like to tuck up in the middle of the night; she might get jealous.'

'I'm sure she'll survive.' Helen turned, determined that this evening would not end in another defeat. 'Shall we go?'

He waved her to the door, watching her with quick intelligence, accurately gauging her mood and deciding whether to go along with it or not. Deciding not to, he waited until she was in the Land Rover before disturbing the peace.

'I rang Terri Donovan today and broke the news of our engagement. I said we'd be in Edinburgh next week if she wanted to do some PR work. We might as well get it all over with at once. I told my agent this morning. One Press conference should do it; that way we don't have them following us about.'

'Rick,' she burst out in protest, 'why don't you consult me before you take things into your own hands? I thought I made it clear when you made your appearance at the nightclub that I didn't appreciate your tactics.'

Unmoved, he started up the Land Rover, urging it forward over the bumpy track. 'Nothing's going to break until next week. You were never going to feel comfortable with the idea; consultation just means pointless arguments over something I have already decided.' He cast her a challenging glance. 'I can't see what you're getting so steamed up about. If it weren't for me you'd still be linked with that creep, Michael Burton.'

Her laughter echoed disbelief. 'Are you trying to tell me I should be grateful? You've used every dirty trick imaginable to get me to play this twisted game of yours. Don't pretend you're doing me any favours.'

His mouth curled into a smile, and it didn't need a genius to work out what he was thinking.

'If I could get away from you you wouldn't see me for dust,' she responded to his unspoken thoughts.

'Oh, I'm sure you'd run,' he agreed solemnly. 'A strong, satisfying relationship scares you to death. Fortunately I'm bigger, braver and a lot faster than you are. It's about time you let a man soak up all that latent sexuality you blast towards a camera. No wonder your viewing figures were high; I watched the tapes of a couple of programmes you did for *Catch the Sun.* You made Bradford look like the place to be.'

Regarding him with resentment, she moved as close to the passenger door as possible to distance herself from him, curiosity prompting her to scrutinise his dark profile. 'The series ended a month ago—how did you get hold of the videos?'

'I have a lot of friends in the so-called "right places".' He gestured to the dark thunder clouds piling up around the castle. 'We're in for a storm. There's always a price for good weather in the Hebrides. I hope you've brought a toothbrush.'

Helen acknowledged that she might need one. The good weather of the last few days had deteriorated into a hot, clammy, breathless waiting. The birds had become strangely silent in the way of storms, and the sheep that moved did so in a way that suggested a growing anxiety.

Castealcreag was welcoming, but the storm had made its own demands and Andy was busy seeing to the shutters of the windows out on the north and south terraces. Sarah was with James in the drawing-room; she looked up as they came in, a smile making her look far younger than the more strained expression worn during her pregnancy.

'Andy tells me congratulations are in order. I wondered why the fridge was crammed with champagne.'

'The champagne is to welcome Helen into the family as well as Janet.' James brought Helen a fluted glass, kissing her cheek and smiling at her with pleasure.

'Isn't getting engaged rather old-fashioned in showbiz circles?' Sarah eyed her brother with sardonic humour. 'I wouldn't have thought it was your style at all.'

'At least you acknowledge I have style; you must be softening,' Rick fenced artfully, deflecting his sister's probing.

'Is Janet in bed?' Helen broke in, convinced that the evening was going to be an uncomfortable one and, unlike Rick, she had no desire to pit her wits against Sarah or anyone else.

'Yes. Mary's giving her a bath and getting her ready for bed to give me a rest. I'll take you up after dinner if you like. She's an angel when she's asleep, but a demon at bathtime.'

Helen smiled, giving Rick a speaking glance. He stonewalled her with a blank look of incomprehension. She knew, to her cost, he could charm the birds off the trees when he wanted to but clearly he had no intention of exercising such skills on his sister. Neither of them seemed willing to give up those childhood battles. Angus Frazer's legacy to his children had not been a benevolent one; each had suffered in some way from the expectations of the dominant, single-minded man. It was those inherited traits in Rick that troubled her. James, too, had a gentle stubbornness that frustrated Cathy Ferguson, and Sarah had the burden of belonging to a despised sex to contend with.

When they sat down to dinner the storm was already to be heard, rumbling around out at sea, sheet lightning making the sky glimmer. Helen swallowed drily; she had never quite been able to subdue her fear of storms. She didn't eat very much of the game soup or the pheasant terrine that followed.

'Don't you like storms, darling?' Rick picked up on her tension and she flashed him a surprised look.

'Does anybody?'

'I do,' he replied, the candlelight catching his eyes and revealing the flash of blue in the hooded darkness of his gaze.

'I suppose it's the grand drama that appeals to you,' Sarah chipped in, glancing from one to the other.

'They're not much fun at sea,' Andy commented, not seeming to have much of an appetite either.

James began an anecdote about being caught out in a storm when he was camping on Skye, and smoothly filled in any silences without, Helen guessed, even thinking about it. Rick continued to watch her with predatory sensuality, his eyes following her wine glass to her mouth with an intensification of interest that made her kick him under the table. His affected wince made Andy Frazer fight to keep his mouth straight. Sarah gave an exasperated tut and James continued, unabashed, the twinkle in his eyes the only suggestion that he had an inkling of what was going on.

After dinner Helen accompanied Sarah up to the nursery. For once she wished Rick would join them, but he had remained in the drawing-room with the other two men, talking business, no doubt.

Sarah stood beside the cot, a gentle smile lightening her face as Helen enthused over the small figure snuggled up inside it.

'She's got auburn hair.' Helen sent Sarah a smiling glance, only to feel her smile waver at the knowledgeable glint in the other woman's eyes.

'I suppose you're pregnant. It's the only thing that would make Rick consider marriage. He's determined to better Father in everything.' She saw Helen's baffled expression and sighed. 'I think you're probably genuine, but it's better to know the truth. My mother can't have been happy, knowing Father was having an affair with some gypsy of an actress. Rick's mother pretends she was an innocent girl, seduced by an older man, instead of an actress with a stage-door admirer, which was the way it really was.'

Helen felt her blood run cold. 'You're saying...' Of course! It made sense. Rick had said he had grown up in the States. She had never suspected that his parentage differed from that of James and Sarah, because the picture of the three of them on the boat had rooted them in her mind as a united family.

'Father married her later, when mother died, to legitimise Rick. He thought the world of him, but Rick was poisoned by Sylvia Cameron. She hated the island. I don't even remember her. She didn't wait long to head back to the bright lights. If I were you I'd thrash the whole thing out; I wouldn't become part of Rick's vendetta with the past.'

Was there any truth in what Sarah had said? Had Helen's lack of experience brought back echoes of his mother's dilemma? Was Rick righting his father's wrongs in some ongoing battle to prove himself the better man? Or was he protecting his past from the Press? She felt she still didn't have the whole picture, but it was beginning to make more sense.

'No one appears to want the past to rest,' she commented more to herself than Sarah.

'It can't. Not here. Unlike city life, our identity stretches back over time. If you talk to any of Fiona MacSween's kin you'll find yours does too.'

'Hush, now, that's a lot of noise; you'll wake the child.' Mary MacInnes bustled in, dimming the light and looking into the cot with a gentle smile.

Sarah drew away, nodding as Mary MacInnes told her details of the feed. Helen returned to the drawing-room with her mind in turmoil, wincing as a crack of thunder resounded overhead.

Castealcreag had delighted her during the preparations for the ceilidh. Who couldn't be impressed by the granite edifice with its turreted walls, its indomitable face looking west? Now it seemed steeped in intrigue and mystery. The past wouldn't rest. It imposed its presence even when its progeny escaped the shores of their island home. Clara MacSween had left and spent the rest of her life in a personal feud against the harshness island life imposed. Rick had made his life in Los Angeles but had continued an argument with his father beyond the grave.

'Your mother called.' Rick turned to acknowledge her as she entered the room. 'She wants you to get back to her. Use the study,' he invited, taking in the shadowed worries her eyes revealed. He made to follow her but she put up a hand, staying him.

She felt too disturbed by Sarah's revelations to talk to Rick at that moment. He was too attuned to her moods, and his interrogative skills would tear apart any barriers she cared to put up in minutes. Why did she feel so hurt? She should be delighted that, at last, she had something to threaten him with. Even if she hadn't found all the missing pieces to the jigsaw, she could see enough of the picture to counter his attempts to blackmail her into the Edinburgh Press conference. Escape from his clutches should bring a sense of elation, not this overwhelming feeling of depression.

The study's mullioned windows showed the sea, boiling against the rocks below. Lightning ripped the sky apart, blinding her for a moment. When she could see again it was as if scales had dropped from her eyes.

'I love him,' she said quietly to herself. 'How did that happen?' The question was rhetorical; she, least of all, could answer it. The moment she had met Rick Cameron there had been a sense of familiarity, a fear, an attraction, a knowledge of imminent danger. She had escaped, merely to find herself captive the moment he had arrived on Cladach and accused her of attempting a journalistic scoop.

Whatever Rick's motivation, she was sure he didn't return her feelings. She had always known that his emotions were not rooted in her but in the circumstances

surrounding their relationship. The fact that he derived
pleasure from their affair did little to comfort her. What
was she going to do? She was in love with Rick Cameron,
almost certainly having his baby—she faced the issue
rather than tucking it in some corner at the back of her
mind—but found the idea of being trapped in wedlock
with him frightening. Pride refused to allow her feelings
to pay submission to the past; she had to find a way to
fight in the battle she knew was to come.

Moira Howard sounded guilty, and she hurried
through the admission that Michael Burton had dropped
into their Hampstead home on the pretext of wanting
to contact Helen.

'He seemed to know about Cladach. Well, he said that
he was surprised you enjoyed getting away from it all
and that he had always thought you a city bird. I'm sorry,
Helen, but I let it slip out where you were. It wasn't until
Gilbert said that Burton would have contacted Terri if
he had wanted to get in touch that I realised he might
have ulterior motives.'

Helen swallowed drily. Michael Burton had been
severely discomfited by the Press exposure following
Helen's withdrawal from the contenders for *Option
Three*. Then, when some kind of compromise had been
patched, Rick had promised to flatten him if he tried
any further form of sexual harassment. For a man who
prided himself on being a smooth operator, the circumstances surrounding his involvement with Helen
Howard had been less than satisfactory. He had reason
to hate both herself and Rick, and what fitting pun-
ishment to send the Press hounds into their sanctuary!

'It can't be helped.' She tried to comfort her mother,
whom she could tell felt she had let the side down. 'Did
you say anything about Rick . . . being one of the Frazer
family?'

The silence on the other end told her what she wanted
to know. Biting her lip, she accepted that she had done

just what Rick feared. Her presence had exposed his family to the public revelations he had tried so hard to avoid.

She sat there for a long time, just staring out into the storm. Strangely the destructive power she had always feared provided a necessary catharsis for her troubled mind. The door opened and she felt Rick's presence without seeing him.

'Something wrong?'

She turned to look at him, her green eyes wary. 'Michael Burton knows where we are.' She revealed the circumstances her mother had quoted and let him draw similar conclusions to her own.

'Damn!' A muscle worked in Rick's jaw. He stood near the window, dark brows drawn, his eyes brooding over the seascape. 'We'll have to move the Edinburgh Press conference forward,' he decided, catching her surprised look with a mocking appraisal. 'We're news. We'll give them what they want. If we feed them enough they'll become satiated. Mystery makes news, darling. If we tell them that we both disappeared because we were so much in love that nothing else mattered it will let Burton off the hook, and hopefully he'll crawl back under the stone he came from.'

'No,' she refused. 'I don't want any more of this——'

Rick didn't move, but her eyes widened at the dark threat he embodied. 'You've suddenly become very brave. I could just as easily distract the Press with a sob-story; remember that.'

'We could give them a field-day,' she agreed, her face white with strain. 'When I tell them I can't marry you because you don't love me and you're just trying to put right the wrongs your father did to your mother we should be plastered over the front page for weeks.'

'Well, haven't you been busy?' His tone was scathing, and she felt a *frisson* of fear run from the tip of her toes to her scalp. Standing up, she tried to move away as he came closer, but he was too quick for her, grasping her shoulders, his eyes dark and demanding in the gloom. 'Running away again, Helen? It's getting to be a pointless exercise, don't you think? You can't run away from me, because I won't let you.'

It was hardly lover-like; it sounded more like a threat.

'No. . .' she whispered, panic growing as his intention became clear.

Bending his head, he touched his mouth to hers, following the slight movement away she attempted before consuming the tremulous curves in a slow, consciously erotic kiss. Helen felt naked under the assault of her new and intense emotions. He made her body his ally with such wicked exploitation of his own sexual power. Drawing her up against him, her eyes pleading with him, he gathered up the bright gold of her hair, twisting it around one fist. Her green eyes were as stormy and hectic as the sea pounding below them. Her lips were slightly parted as if awaiting the penetration of his tongue. Obligingly he ran the tip over her lower lip, sinking deeply into the soft warmth within, and felt the clutch of her fingers against his shoulders under the dark material of his jacket.

'So willing,' he murmured smokily when he had reduced her to clinging to him, her golden head resting against his chest, her face turned into the hand that stroked her cheek. 'So warm and so stubborn. You think you can turn back to your sterile existence in London and not need this. Ever since we first made love you've tried to limit the damage, but it hasn't worked. If you lasted a week your sleep would be wrecked, and every corner you turned you'd be looking for me.'

Helen recalled her meandering walk through London's parkland following her row with Rick the night of the *Option Three* promotion. She had found him then and had allowed herself to be persuaded into lunch and had responded to him so mindlessly in the car on the way back. She had berated herself afterwards for being so gullible, but it came to her with glaring simplicity that she had been only too willing to be persuaded.

It was on the tip of Helen's tongue to suggest he might not be the only male to exert such power over her, but, since it was patently untrue and she suspected he would make her suffer for the challenge, she decided to err on the side of discretion.

'If it makes it any easier...' he rubbed his thumb over her cheekbone '...it's not me I'm asking you to help protect. You know about my parentage—I presume Sarah filled you in on the details.' Her eyes told him the answer, and he nodded resignedly. 'My mother has re-married recently to a Henry Knowles. He strongly disapproves of divorce and assumes she's a widow. The circumstances surrounding my birth and her divorce from Angus Frazer would not exactly make his day. Having it spread luridly over his morning paper might well threaten the marriage.' Regarding her steadily, he watched her absorb the information. 'I need your help, Helen.'

'It took a long time for you to ask!' she pointed out heatedly.

'I prefer to be in control. Depending on other people can be a risky business. Besides——' his thumb moved to the corner of her mouth, and resentment flared into life, her eyes as brilliant as emeralds '—you were too busy trying to restore the barricades to help me out voluntarily.'

Pulling away, she turned her back on him, trying to think. Helen felt helpless in the face of circumstance. She felt responsible for making Rick and his mother victims of Michael Burton's vindictive campaign against her.

'All right.' She turned back to him, daring him to look triumphant. 'If you promise not to touch me again.'

'Helen——'

'I want your promise.' She was determined, and it showed in her eyes and the tilt of her chin.

Rick sighed heavily, his expression full of mockery. 'You drive a hard bargain.'

'Is it agreed?'

Something primitive flared in his eyes, but it was almost immediately subdued and he nodded. 'Much as it pains my masculine ego, I'll leave it to you to make the next move.'

Helen tried to pretend she wouldn't be the least tempted. She didn't want him to draw those shattering words of love from her, and if she hadn't had his promise to stay away she felt he would use the weapons of persuasion he possessed to do just that. He was ruthless in his pursuit of her secrets as if taking them away from her made him safe.

When they returned to the drawing-room James was alone, smoking his pipe, and he greeted them with warm speculation in his eyes.

Rick filled him in on the Michael Burton threat and his intention to spike the other man's guns by making a public announcement.

'You must do as you think best, Rick. You know more about the media than I do. I suspect if you hand them a fairy-tale they might enjoy trying to destroy it.'

'They might. But it will keep them occupied.'

'Will you stay a while, Rick? I want to discuss the plans for the hotel with you.'

He invited Helen to join them, but she wasn't capable of polite conversation and expressed her intention to accept their hospitality and go to bed.

She had been given the same guest room as before, and the evening's events and the memories of the first time she had stayed in that room kept her from sleep. The storm had diminished to a low growl, the sea's thrash losing its violence, the eternal sound of waves breaking on stone settling into a regular rhythm.

For the first time since they had met Helen felt as if she was on an equal footing in her relationship with Rick. She had agreed to help him, and he in turn had agreed to halt his piratical attitude to physical intimacy. If she was pregnant, she realised, they would become embroiled in battle once more. The thought made her utterly weary, and she fell into sleep with a heavy heart. Would she never escape this man...and did she really want to?

CHAPTER NINE

'I WISH this were all over!' Helen moved agitatedly around the room, observed with interest by her agent.

'For a media personality, you don't think much of the spotlight,' Terri reflected on what to her was a paradoxical quirk in the other woman's make-up. 'I bet the dazzling Mr Cameron isn't losing his cool. That man just basks in the limelight.'

Helen glanced at her watch. It was ten minutes to blast-off, and her composure was in shreds. The last time the Press had taken any interest in her private life she had felt totally invaded. Now, for the sake of Rick's mother, she was going through it all again.

'You can always call it off. Or does Svengali call the shots?'

The quick shift of attention to her agent was arresting, and Terri Donovan took a deep breath. 'Did I stand on someone's toes?'

Helen looked away again. When she was out of Rick's influence she did wonder how he managed to talk her into seeing things his way. 'Svengali' was an apt enough title.

'This is simpler than having reporters follow us wherever we go. You want to try it and see how much you like it.' She maintained the pretence with difficulty.

'I can't think why they'd want to visit some remote Scottish island. If I were following the rich and famous I'd make sure they were heading for the Riviera.'

Helen's smile was a mere travesty, adequately sketching the state of her feelings.

'When are you getting married? They're sure to ask.'

147

Helen looked startled. 'I—er—we haven't set a date yet.'

'And I thought you were in a hurry.' Terri Donovan gave her a cunning look. 'I bet Rick Cameron has thought about it. He's been through enough of these to write their questions for them.'

Helen groaned inwardly. They had discussed the story they were to give to the Press, and the fact that Rick hadn't discussed the possibility of being asked to give a date for the wedding was unusually remiss of him. Unless he had some devious motive for leaving her in ignorance. What could he possibly gain . . . ? She was half addled when he exerted his sexual magnetism over her; it robbed her of her common sense in a way she had yet to get used to.

The conversation she had with Sarah stirred in her memory. He hadn't asked her about the possibility that she was pregnant for some time, although he had mentioned it in passing when manoeuvring her over the engagement business. But surely he wouldn't tie himself down by committing himself to a date? He was an international film star, with women throwing themselves at him left, right and centre; he didn't have to trap anyone into marriage. Forewarned was forearmed; she was probably getting paranoid, but if he had some twisted reason to complicate their situation further she would have to make sure he didn't succeed.

Viewing herself in the mirror of the hotel room they had hired, she surveyed her face dispassionately. Her hair swept down her back, its gold teased into loose ringlets. Her eyebrows were darker, so too her lashes, giving the green eyes depth in a way that one woman's magazine had described as 'keeping secrets'. She had a straight, small, model's nose, her mouth generous, but none of the features that made up her face looked different. It was something beyond the grasp of description; her body proclaimed her a woman in a way that separated her from the Helen Howard of yesterday. He had changed her, the thought struck her. Without him as a reference, she was an alien in her own body. It was frightening how much she needed him. His promise to refrain from physical intimacy had been hard won, but being in proximity and not touching with the high-voltage sexuality that crackled between them was a torture all on its own.

'Time's nearly up.' Terri Donovan watched her curiously, knowing that the close inspection had little to do with vanity. Out of all the stars or would-be stars in her stable, she liked Helen the most. It was probably because she was the one least addicted to her own image. She didn't know what created the tension she sensed in Helen, but almost expected her to make a problem about what other women would consider a dream come true. Rick Cameron was going to be one of the acting greats. He was a real man, if such a thing existed, the sort of man that made much-loved husbands or boyfriends dim in allure just by casting a glance. Wasn't it just typical of Helen Howard to have such a man pursuing her and regard it as something of a problem?

'I'm ready.' Taking a slow, deep breath, Helen drew upon internal reservoirs of pride. It wasn't an execution. She was just going to tell the world she was in love and hope that that would be the end of it. Smoothing her hands over the gold suede skirt she wore with matching jacket that, apart from the soft material, was an aggressive combination of zips and buckles, she flexed her shoulders and prepared to enter the arena.

The Press conference reminded her of those held for competing heavy-weight boxers, each coming on from different camps to the explosion of flashlight. Meeting Rick's gaze, she knew the battle was just as real, and she felt her spine stiffening. This was her world, too, not just his. She had been in front of the camera since her teens and wasn't going to be hustled into anything. 'Meet your match, Mr Cameron,' her eyes told him, and for a moment some ineffable emotion flickered back at her that she didn't understand.

The circus began. The story for the most part mirrored the truth except that Rick claimed they had met in Edinburgh, where he had stayed to gain some familiarity with the location of his new film. He revealed that she had a cottage on the Hebridean island where his father's family lived and they had renewed their acquaintance when he had visited his relatives.

'Was it love at first sight?' a prominent gossip columnist, Lisa West, asked sweetly.

'Something close.' Rick's arm slid around her shoulders and she gave him a speaking look as the cameras went into a frenzy.

Rick, she noted, while admitting his Scottish links, had dressed in a decidedly American fashion. He wore a pale blue denim shirt and jeans, a white vest T-shirt showing at his collar, his dark hair springy and vital. He could have stepped out of a Levi's advert.

'You're not helping,' he murmured into her ear.

'Sorry, I thought it was a virtuoso performance.' She batted her eyelashes at him.

'Quite a change in direction for you.' The same journalist turned her attention to Helen. 'There were rumours linking your name with Michael Burton's.'

'The Press don't always get it right, do they?' She was a far better journalist than Lisa West and could also turn on the saccharin when she chose. 'As far as I'm aware, Michael Burton is happily married and intends to stay that way.' She felt like saying she wouldn't touch the greasy little toad with a barge-pole, but diplomacy forbade it.

'So when's the wedding date?' a heavy-jowled hack broke in. 'Soon?'

'We haven't set a date yet.' Helen leant forward at exactly the right time and prevented any attempt by Rick to give a more positive answer.

'Any ideas, Rick?' The Press scented discord.

'Tomorrow would suit me. It depends on the lady.'

The lady remained evasive. The conference ended with calls for a kiss. Helen met his lips coolly, determined not to feel a thing, and almost succeeded.

Terri Donovan winked at her in a conspiratorial fashion as Rick approached to claim her, and disappeared on to her next engagement.

Grasping her wrist, Rick led her out through a back entrance thoughtfully guarded by the hotel staff, and didn't speak until they were in the screened limousine waiting to take them to the airport.

'What was that about?' he exploded. 'We're supposed to announce the love-affair of the decade, and you come on as if we're on different sides of a war.'

'We haven't decided a date,' she pointed out. 'I didn't want you to say something you might regret.' Taking a deep breath, she decided it was time to give herself some space and test out what Rick Cameron's motives actually were. 'I...I'm not pregnant. I...well, I'm not...' She avoided going into technical details. 'Engagements can be broken, but if we set a date the Press would be back in a matter of weeks or months, wouldn't they? I really can't see how setting a date would have helped.'

If she had expected him to look overcome with relief, or passionately declare his undying love, she was to be disappointed on both counts. Rick Cameron's face was cast in bronze with about as much emotion as cold metal.

'So, assuming we've assuaged public interest, where do we go from here? I want you in my life, Helen——'

'You want me in your bed.' She was chill.

His eyes were heavily lidded as he regarded her, scenting her fear and puzzled by it as much as it maddened him. 'And you, of course, don't want to be there?' His tone was as dry as a desert. He released her from his gaze, turning to look out of the window at the

cosmopolitan Princes Street. 'Do you want to end our
relationship, or are we going to continue with this dance
routine where you play Red Riding Hood to my Big Bad
Wolf?'

Hurt by his unforthcoming attitude, she viewed his
profile, wishing that she could listen to his thoughts.
'Does it matter to you? Or am I just the most alluring
woman on the island while you do your tour of duty?'

His mouth twisted in disgust, and when he turned to
her his eyes glittered with sheer fury. 'I told you when
we met that you made a refreshing change from all those
blowsy little starlets trying to boost their careers. Virgins
are a rare breed these days; you added a touch of spice
to an otherwise dull diet...' He caught her wrist as she
hit him, pushing the attacking hand back against the
leather upholstery. 'You're an ambitious lady; why don't
you jump down from that lofty pedestal you've put
yourself on? I've got a lot of contacts in American television. That ice and fire act you've perfected would make
you a hot property with the right exposure.'

'I'd sweep the streets before I accepted any help from
you!' She gazed up at him, her rage matching his, her
green eyes glittering with hostility.

'Brave words,' he sneered. 'When you're desperate
enough you can crawl into my bed and I might just let
you stay. In the meantime we stay engaged to repair the
damage you and your mother have done between you,
until I say differently.'

'And if I disagree?' she fought him back, anger an-
aesthetising pain.

'You won't.' He made the assertion sound like the
threat it undoubtedly was. 'Unless you want to join Clara
MacSween as the second member of your family exiled
from the island.' He witnessed the indignation in her
eyes and smiled nastily. 'Just try me. One word to Murdo
and you won't get any more supplies for the shop. Being

a Frazer means something on Cladach. Believe me, I make a bad enemy.'

Helen did believe him. She subsided into a silence underscored by bitter pain. So much for the brief truce. It hadn't taken him long to revert back to form and use threats instead of depending on her help. Now that he no longer had the threat of Press exposure to keep her in his power he was using every despicable tactic he could think of to bend her to his will. Some small part of her wished she had remained truthful and not attempted to reveal the emotional depths of their relationship. As far as she knew, she was still having his child, and as time continued to tick by the possibility of an aberration in her cycle became less and less likely.

The journey back to Cladach was a nightmare. They hardly spoke. He deposited her back at Samhrad Taigh and returned to the helicopter without saying goodbye. Helen sought the warmth of the island home, and threw herself on to the bed and burst into tears. It had all gone horribly wrong!

The newspapers that came over with Murdo the next day didn't improve the situation. All homed in on her hesitance to name the date, and put Rick Cameron in the role of ardent suitor in pursuit of an evasive lady.

'He won't like that,' she muttered to herself, and looked up into James Frazer's twinkling blue eyes and blinked with surprise. It wasn't often he came into the shop without being helped out of the Land Rover. She hadn't heard the engine, and her curiosity grew as Cathy came in behind him.

'Are you in today's paper?' James enquired. 'There was a short snippet at the end of the news last night. Rick's as cross as a bear. What have you done to him?'

'It was a bad day.' She shrugged dismissively. A sudden smile lit her features. 'You're walking without a stick!'

He chuckled, flattered by her delight. 'For short periods only. It's good to be on the mend. I'm going to

visit the distillery and Cathy said you hadn't seen it yet.
She's kindly offered to mind the shop while I repair the
oversight.'

'Oh. That's very kind, but I should really be giving
Cathy a rest; she's virtually been running the shop since
Aunt Fi died.'

'Nonsense. It's no trouble. Besides, I've seen the distillery many times. James is determined to go, so he might
as well have company.' Giving Helen her car keys, Cathy
refused to let James Frazer drive, commenting that
walking was enough strain on his newly knit bones.

Feeling that she was being manoeuvred but not sure
why, Helen agreed. She drove the battered Ford Escort
over to the west coast of the island to where the distillery
was sited, near the banks of a peaty burn. James, as
good as his word, showed her the copper stills, explaining that they had to be emptied every time the
process was complete. Malting the barley, he revealed,
was a method by which the moist grains were warmed
and then dried by peat smoke to ensure that the starches
turned to sugar. He went on to discuss the Islay whiskies
and the differences in flavour, but the technicalities of
a good malt were beyond Helen, so she just nodded politely and asked the occasional, hopefully intelligent,
question.

'I've bored you enough.' James grinned at her protest
and took her arm, leading her through to the office,
which had a wonderful view of the burn and the heather-
clad hills around them. Behind the desk was the eagle
and thistle emblem raised in plaster on the wall. Portraits
occupied much of the wall space, and James pointed out
the picture of Malcolm Frazer, who had caused Clara
MacSween's exile, and then that of his own father, Angus
Frazer. Both the men had chosen to be painted in traditional costume, neither face giving a picture of the real
man. James and Sarah resembled Frazer stock, but, apart

from the sensual cast of the mouth, Rick was nothing like them.

'I suppose I'll go up there eventually.' He gave a rueful grimace. 'It should really be Rick. He stopped us being swallowed up by one of the brewing giants by establishing links in America. He's virtually looked after marketing and advertising ever since. He oversees distribution in the States,' he informed her. 'He has a permanent team over there for that very purpose.'

Green eyes met blue. 'And?'

'Am I that transparent?' James appeared to be grateful when a young man knocked at the door and brought in some coffee. 'Thank you, Hamish.' He waited for the door to close before continuing. 'I may be wrong, and I hope you'll excuse me for interfering, but it seems to me that you might have got the impression that Rick is undependable in some way.' Handing her a mug of coffee, he was quite serious in his defence of his brother. 'I know Sarah blames him for my accident, but really Rick had no choice. A car was coming straight at us, having overtaken on a bend. It was a miracle he kept control of the car. We were very lucky to come off as lightly as we did.'

Helen warmed her hand on her mug of coffee. The distillery was obviously a male domain—no secretary with china cups here.

'I think I rejected Sarah's version of events a long time ago—it isn't that, James.' She sipped her coffee, aware of his expectant silence. 'We've had a row, as I'm sure you've gathered. At the moment Rick's terms for a reconciliation are a little too harsh.' Her humour didn't quite make it to her eyes, but she smiled bravely under James's kind and watchful gaze.

'He'll come round,' he predicted reassuringly. 'He's still a bit of a hothead, but his temper burns out quickly.' The phone's ringing broke into the conversation, and he picked up the receiver, a deep frown creasing his brow as he spoke rapidly in Gaelic to whoever was on the other end. He was standing before he had put the receiver back in place.

'Sounds as though we're in for another storm. Sarah's worried because Andy's boat hasn't returned. Och, he's not a man to take risks; he'll find shelter and ride it out.'

She followed him to the car, a quick glance at the sky revealing that the storm of the night before seemed to be returning, the sky ominously dark over the hills. 'Is there anything I can do?'

'If you see a boat, light the beacon at Cladach Bagh.' His blue eyes twinkled. 'That's what they used to do to guide the fishermen back home. Andy will be fine. Sarah's bound to panic; she's still weak from having the baby.'

Rick was in the courtyard of Caste`alcreag when they arrived, his eyes hard as he swept over the car and Helen in particular. Hauling on a waxed jacket, he came over to speak to James.

'I'll go out as far as I can. Andy won't stay out at sea unless he's got engine trouble...'

'I'll come with you.' She offered Rick her help, but he shook his head.

'You'd get in the way.' He was abrupt. 'It won't be a pleasure cruise with the storm building.'

'Be careful.' She couldn't help the words spilling from her lips. Rick glanced over his shoulder but said nothing.

James didn't see the flash of pain in her eyes, too busy himself with organising the coastal watch. They would all be involved; she felt a lump come to her throat. All equal in their concern. One of their own was missing, and they would maintain their vigil until the lost boat returned.

She was offered a lift back to Samhrad Taigh and decided to take it. Mary MacInnes was with Sarah, and the idea persisted that Cladach Bagh would be the starting-point for Rick's search. However illusory the sense of closeness would be, she instinctively felt the cottage was where she should be.

The wind picked up imperceptibly at first, and then it began to buffet the windows of the cottage, the sky pewter-grey, the light fading despite its being only five o'clock. Helen didn't know very much about helicopters, but the flimsy construction did not seem to be built for the wildness of the elements promised that night.

Darts of rain bounced off the glass, the wind throwing vicious tantrums around the cottage as if it were the very centre of the storm. Helen looked out towards the sea, willing the sound of helicopter blades to pass overhead. It was then she saw the flash, like a firework in the sky. She jumped to her feet and froze, staring hard into the growing darkness.

The beacon! She might make herself the laughing-stock of the island, but that didn't matter. If, for some reason, Andy's boat was making for Cladach Bagh they would have the fire to guide them.

With cool precision she marvelled at later she piled firelighters, dry wood sticks, and a plastic container full of paraffin into a rucksack and took anything she could carry that would burn.

It was almost a mile to the bay and the weather tore at her cagoule, the road barely visible and disintegrating into a rutted path of mud in places. More than once she lost her footing, and on one occasion the wind caught her and she was hurled into the waiting arms of a gorse bush. Its spiky branches tore at her hands and clothes, one thorn scratching her forehead just above her eyebrow.

The mud caked her jeans, water cascading down from her weather-proof jacket to ensure they were absolutely sodden. It was like some terrible nightmare. She could hardly see. Her hearing was full of the sound of the wind thrashing the gorse and heather.

She found the site for the beacon purely by accident. Her task seemed futile. How was she going to make anything burn long enough to be seen out at sea? A sheer desire for shelter made her stumble a short way down the path leading to the sea. The wind blew her back against a small recess in the cliff face. It didn't quite have cave status, but it was protected from the worst of the rain and wind. Her foot hit metal and she found a contraption that resembled the braziers she could remember workmen using. Quickly she emptied her small store of fuel into the drum and took out the paraffin, her hands almost too numb to unscrew the top.

Another flash of light came from the sea, closer this time, and she struck a match and stood back quickly as the paraffin exploded into flame. For a moment she was amazed at her own success, then she began to look around for material to burn. Several half-burnt logs were scattered about. There were one or two cans littering the ground and she guessed it was one of the places where the adolescents of the island met out of sight of their parents. Dragging one of the hefty pieces of timber across to the brazier, she almost died of fright when a piece of wood clanged into it, seemingly of its own volition.

'It wouldn't occur to you to call.' Rick, soaked to the skin, heaved the piece of wood she had been struggling with into the brazier to join the other. 'Stay here.' His tone brooked no refusal. 'Hamish . . .' The rest was in Gaelic but she could see the light of torches and hear a mixture of voices. Hamish stayed behind to help keep the fire alive.

'Their engine failed. Andy managed to patch it up, but the storm had got up by then. Rick guided them in but had to do an emergency landing. He put the helicopter down near Roin Bagh and phoned from your cottage.'

Helen nodded. She should have done that. She had been in such an almighty panic to get the beacon lit that the simple expediency of a phone call had gone out of her mind.

'You got the beacon lit,' the young man's soft voice congratulated her. 'Hopefully you've kept them off the rocks. No one could have done that more quickly.'

Her face was too stiff to smile her thanks to the young islander. She moved near to the fire, glad of its warmth, her eyes narrowed, trying to see a glimpse of the boat. It must have been one of the longest hours of her life.

She was weak with relief when bowed figures with blankets round their shoulders made their way up the path. Hamish's jubilant shout told her all she wanted to know.

'Oh, thank God,' she whispered, her teeth chattering over the small words of thanks.

Stiffly she joined the group of bedraggled individuals and found her wrist grasped in a no-nonsense manner; then she was half dragged up the remaining path to the waiting Land Rover. Another car moved off in front of them and she was aware of Niall Ferguson at the wheel, while Rick held her firmly against him to avoid the worst of the bumps the suspension couldn't eradicate.

It felt blissful to be out of the storm and relieved of the worry over Andy and Rick. It was nice being held by Rick Cameron, who was compromised into being pleasant by Niall Ferguson's presence.

'Some headline this is going to make,' Rick muttered with sardonic humour.

'I'm sick of headlines.' She felt tears well up in her eyes.

'So am I,' Rick muttered grimly, wiping her face with a white handkerchief the distillery manager passed over at his request. 'How long ago did you have a tetanus shot?'

'Last year,' she murmured.

The Land Rover slowed down as it approached Castealcreag. The courtyard seemed to hold every car on the island. Sarah rushed out to embrace her husband, tears streaming down her face.

When Rick got out of the Land Rover and insisted on lifting Helen out there was a ripple of applause from the figures hidden within waxed jackets and cagoules. Soft Gaelic words of thanks and praise surrounded them. Helen felt tears run down her cheeks and she looked up into Rick's eyes, which held a glitter of admiration.

'I can't exile you now.' He spoke for her ears only. 'I'd have a riot on my hands.'

Cathy Ferguson appeared as they entered the castle. Assessing the situation, she said she'd run them both a hot bath. Taking Helen up the stairs, Rick took her into his suite. Stripping the jacket off her, he was careful when releasing her hands.

'I think you've got half the moor on you,' he muttered, undoing the zip of her jeans and easing them down her thighs. Cathy could be heard moving around in the bathroom. Finding his bathrobe, Rick wrapped it around her bedraggled figure.

As he crouched beside where she sat on his bed a glint of reluctant amusement came into his eyes.

'I know I look a fright.' She was immediately defensive, unaware of the rumpled fragility she exuded that was infinitely appealing. 'You don't look so hot yourself. You'd better take off those wet things.'

She could feel the cold from his skin, and drops of water were still dripping from his hair, dark lashes narrowed, his eyes as black as the storm outside. 'Are you flirting with me, Miss Howard?' His voice held a husky note that made her go weak at the knees.

'I wouldn't dream of it, Mr Cameron.' Her tone was light, but she accepted the intimate depth of his gaze, a stirring of warmth bringing her cold skin tinglingly alive.

'Want to help?' He smiled at the echoes of shock she couldn't hide. Pushing off the waxed jacket, he showed her his hands, which were raw with exposure. 'I don't know if I can manage my shirt.'

The shirt was scarlet tartan with stud fastenings, tucked into jeans as wet as her own.

'You seemed to manage when you were undressing me,' she pointed out, realising she was getting perilously close to breaking her own rule on physical intimacy.

'The incentive was greater.' His smile was warm and attractive, and she had Cathy to thank that the situation didn't escalate further.

'The water's ready.' She paused on the threshold, glancing from one to the other, clearly conscious of intruding.

'Rick...' Helen didn't know what she intended to say, but it was difficult to let him go when her emotions were at such a heightened pitch.

Placing a finger against her lips, he regarded her seriously. 'The rules don't change, honey. It's up to you. You know my terms.'

She watched him go. She had annoyed him when she had suggested he was using her to pass his time more pleasantly on the island. No, annoyed wasn't strong enough; she had glimpsed fury in his eyes. He had said he wanted her in his life; she had been the one to denigrate their relationship into mere physical attraction.

It was that old fear, she acknowledged, the fear of taking a risk. The fear of loving someone and losing them. Her eyes became drenched with pain when she remembered sitting in the cottage maintaining her dark vigil. Not saying 'I love you' wouldn't have made the pain any easier if Rick had smashed the helicopter into a cliff. A small, choked cry of distress broke from her lips, and Cathy's movement in the doorway made her look up, something of what she felt still mirrored in her eyes.

'You're tired,' the other girl comforted her. 'It will seem better in the morning.'

Helen nodded. She did feel tired. And she had... the baby—her mind came to terms with the thought—to think of. Pulling the robe around her, she made for the damp heat of the bathroom and let the silky warmth of the water soothe her cold, tired flesh.

CHAPTER TEN

HELEN emerged from the bathroom the next morning, her face pale and wan. She felt absolutely dreadful. She tried to pretend that the events from the night before had upset her stomach, but 'morning sickness' kept popping into her mind to add to the ravages of a poor night's sleep. She gave a start of surprise when she saw Sarah and then went red, which improved her colour considerably.

'I took back the breakfast and brought you tea and some digestives. I found that quite helpful.'

Helen pushed a distracted hand through her hair, the golden silken strands catching the light as they cascaded back into place. She didn't feel well enough to bluff her way out of it.

'It will pass,' Sarah encouraged her with a humorous glint in her eye.

'Are you sure?' Helen looked at the digestives dubiously.

'If you're in any pain I'll get Rick to fetch the doctor...'

'No, no,' Helen replied hastily. 'I just feel queasy, that's all.'

Sarah looked relieved. 'I wouldn't like to think you'd put yourself at risk last night. I can't thank you enough for responding so quickly. Andy says it was a very close-run thing, and he's not one to exaggerate.'

Helen shivered at the thought of what might have been. It all seemed like a dream in the light of morning, but

she had the scratches on her hands and face to prove
that it was true.

'There's a meeting today,' Sarah revealed, watching
the younger woman sip tentatively at the tea. 'I've decided to at least listen to what Rick has to say. There
might be some value in the hotel project, as long as it's
properly supervised,' she added with a touch of her old
fervour.

Helen was stunned, staring at the woman for a moment
and then smiling slowly. 'I'm glad. Rick loves Cladach;
I'm sure he'll listen to your reservations on the subject.'

Sarah pursed her mouth in humorous doubt. 'Listening will be a new experience for both of us.' Standing
up, she viewed Helen with a certain amount of curiosity.
'Have you told him about the baby?'

'I—er—not yet, no.'

'I'll keep quiet, then.' She went to the door, pausing
before she left the room. 'Thank you, Helen. I'm glad
you've kept on Fiona's cottage; I think she would have
been very proud of you.'

Praise indeed, and Helen wasn't immune to a glow of
pleasure. It was a day of thanks and gentle approval.
Wherever Helen went, she was greeted with warmth and
friendliness. She had always been the recipient of
kindness and hospitality on the island, but that had been
a legacy from her Aunt Fi. That day she was accepted
for herself, and a feeling of belonging swept over her.

When she returned to the cottage the feeling of con-
tentment generated by the islanders' thanks dwindled
away. The problems surrounding her relationship with
Rick piled up like huge thunder clouds around her head.
It had seemed all very well to say she wasn't having a
baby, when she had had the brilliant scheme of making
Rick reveal his motives, but it caused a whole new set
of problems when you wanted to tell a man you cared

deeply for him to throw in as a sideline, 'Oh, by the way, I am pregnant after all.'

She must have rehearsed what she was going to say at least twenty times before he put in an appearance, and by that time the effort had exhausted her. It didn't help that his success in getting island approval for the hotel had cloaked him in glittering triumph, and he exuded energy.

'Hard day in the shop?' he greeted her, viewing her prone figure with scant attention. Uncorking a bottle of champagne he had brought with him, he searched for glasses, the streaming liquid fizzing and descending to the carpet. 'They say every cloud has a silver lining. I think Andy's getting caught up in the storm made Sarah think twice about the island's historic dependence on the fishing industry.'

Helen's lip curled. 'It couldn't be that she was grateful for your part in Andy's rescue, could it?' she queried acidly. 'Or the fact that you've impressed her with the way you've helped James and got her to the hospital in time to safely deliver little Janet?'

He considered this and gave a little shrug. 'I suppose we've all changed. Even James. He's showing interest in the distribution of Castealcreag in the States. It would be a good idea to have one of the family over there while I'm based in Edinburgh. It might satiate Cathy's wanderlust. It would be great if they could settle their differences.'

Helen tried not to feel envious. She wished James and Cathy all the joy in the world, but it threw into direct contrast the muddled state of her own love-life.

Handing her a glass of champagne, Rick frowned as if he was seeing her for the first time. 'You look pale.'

'We don't all have your empire-building energy.' The tensions of the night before and having to wait to see him until the evening had made her edgy. She avoided

his eyes when he went down on his haunches beside the
couch. His arm was resting near to her thigh and she
could see each dark individual hair scattered across his
forearm. He had large hands, she mused, but they were
nicely shaped in a manly way. Forcing herself to meet
his gaze, she realised she was transgressing the forbidden boundary that had been erected, and the militant
gleam in her eyes brought the suspicion of a smile to his
lips.

'I think we could both do with a holiday.' His deep,
musical voice gently stirred a well of feeling within her.
She was unaware of the shadow of longing her eyes
communicated. 'I'll make dinner while you think about
it.'

A holiday? She had thought of the island in those
terms, but she reflected that there hadn't been very much
in the way of relaxation since she had set foot on
Cladach.

Sounds of industry were emitted from the kitchen, and
before long the delicious wafts of cooking food made
her realise she had hardly eaten that day. Rick, she decided, was the sort of person that if he was going to do
something he did it well. That explained his many talents
and his absorption in whatever task he chose to focus
on. Halfway through her lobster pancake she learnt the
reason for the elaborate softening up.

'My mother would like to meet you.' Rick casually
introduced the subject, aware of the sudden tension in
her face.

'Is she coming here?' she asked, sounding surprised.

'No way. She makes your grandmother look like a
liberal. She hates the place. You've got another week
before you begin working on *Option Three*. I thought
we could go to California. Have you ever been to Los
Angeles?'

'I've never been to America, full stop,' she informed him, not sure if he was serious.

'Will you come with me?' he requested simply.

She searched his face for a sign of an ulterior motive but found nothing. It was the perfect opportunity to bring up the subject of their ongoing relationship, and yet she quailed at the thought of revealing her deceit. As if sensing her reticence, he didn't push her any further than she was prepared to go.

'Have you told her the truth about our engagement?'

Stroking a finger around her jaw, Rick captured her gaze. 'I don't know the truth about it myself yet. Do you?'

Helen took a deep breath but the words failed her. She didn't want to break off the relationship; she loved him. Feeling as if she was burning her bridges, she agreed to go.

Rick made all the arrangements. Helen found herself packing and being whisked across the Atlantic, not quite sure how she was going to break the deadlock between them but sure that, some time during their week away, it would happen.

California was aptly named the Sunshine State. Everything looked bleached, larger than life. It lived up to its reputation as a vibrant place. Rick claimed that ideas and lifestyles mushroomed daily and were relegated to oblivion just as quickly.

They were greeted at the airport by a uniformed chauffeur who opened the door of a car that seemed to go on forever. The journey to the Knowles home took them through the fairy-tale world of Los Angeles. Their destination, Beverly Hills, was twelve miles west of downtown Los Angeles; it boasted a Hollywood élite and was an elegant and stylish residential area besides possessing in the Golden Triangle a haven for rich, compulsive shoppers.

It was a surprise to find that her hosts lived in a collection of buildings that wouldn't have looked out of place in rural France. Honey-coloured stone and pale grey tiles were the coherent feature of a series of disparate buildings forming a terraced effect as they scaled a hillside. A massive swimming-pool resided at the bottom of the hill, blue and limpid, basking in the golden sunlight.

'Are you sure we're on the right continent?' Helen murmured, and Rick grinned.

'Very Mediterranean, isn't it?' He turned to greet a small dark woman who ran down the steps with sheer delight.

'Oh, Rick, it's so lovely to have you home,' Rick's mother enthused as she was lifted off her feet in a bear-hug. The resemblance between them was striking. Behind her, waiting to be introduced, was Henry Knowles. Rick had told her his mother's husband was involved in banking, and he seemed a pleasant enough man, welcoming them both and talking to Helen when, after a brief hello, Sylvia Knowles turned her attention back to her son.

'I've arranged a party for tomorrow night,' Sylvia enthused when they were seated and a maid had brought in cool drinks. 'I thought tonight you could rest and then we could introduce Helen to your friends, Rick.'

Helen saw Rick's mouth twist slightly but he merely met his mother's dark eyes with a level stare. 'That's nice. But I'd rather you didn't involve us too much in socialising; Helen needs a rest. I want her to soak up some sun and relax before she starts work on her new programme.'

'Of course. Whatever you want.' Sylvia Knowles smiled at him ingenuously. Helen sensed they were very close but could also read each other like a proverbial book. Where Rick was concerned, it was a skill she would like to develop.

Dinner was served by the pool. The temperature had dropped, leaving the evening pleasantly cool. The mixed scents of flowers and shrubs perfumed the air. Ferns and ivy climbed the naturalistic awning made of matting supported by trellis-work. The dining table and chairs were stylish garden furniture, the table decorated by a basic but expensive example of Spanish pottery crammed with sweet peas. Candles flickered in sunken pots, protected from the breeze. Expensive bottles of French wine showed their hosts had good taste as well as money.

Both men wore dinner jackets, and Sylvia dressed in a beautifully cut black velvet two-piece. Helen hadn't missed the welcome 'home' and emphasis on 'friends'. If Sylvia Knowles disliked her son's involvement with the Frazers his intention to devote the coming year to the island while he filmed in Edinburgh was ominous enough, but an engagement to a fellow islander would be a downright threat. Helen decided that now wasn't the time to play the shrinking violet. Dressing in a strapless creation in red shot taffeta that hugged her hips and clung to her thighs, Helen looked very much a hot-house flower rather than a demure English rose.

'That dress is indecent.' Rick took her wrist and viewed her from back and front, before taking her elbow and guiding her to where they were to dine.

'Well, I think you look very nice.' She pouted at him reproachfully and had the satisfaction of seeing his gaze latch on to her mouth.

Sylvia Knowles was expansive about the wonders of LA. 'The shops here are wonderful. Tiffany's, Gucci's, all those places you see in the movies are just here in Beverly Hills. You've never been to the States before, have you, Helen?'

'No; Canada, Mexico and Brazil,' she demurred. 'Oh, yes, Hawaii—I suppose that's counted. One of my co-presenters used to bag the States; I preferred the Orient, so we used to swap assignments. I worked on a travel programme.' She casually took the wind out of Sylvia Knowles's sails.

'How interesting.' Her hostess sounded as if she meant anything but. 'Rick, how on earth could you confine yourself to Edinburgh for a year? It never stops raining. I should know, I was born there.'

'I like Scotland.' He appeared to enjoy the battle taking place between the two women in his life, his smile lazy with amusement. 'It's real.'

'And I suppose Los Angeles isn't!' She gave him a fiery look.

'They don't call it Tinsel Town for nothing.' He winked at her and she laughed. 'If I run out of vitamin D, I'll come here for a fix, OK?'

'You'll come home anyway.' She pointed her fork at him meaningfully and he grinned.

'Yes, Momma.'

'What it is to be wanted,' Helen commented mockingly when he escorted her to her guest cabin later that evening. 'Your mother doesn't like the idea of me very much, does she?'

'Mothers tend to be possessive. Yours isn't too keen on me.' He looked down at her, his dark hair riffled by the wind, his eyes dark and unreadable. 'It's not you, it's Scotland, and the Frazers, the past...' He shrugged. 'Old scars might heal, but they still hurt.'

Helen put up her hand to the side of his face, wanting to take the pain out of those dark memories and wanting...just wanting. She swallowed hard when he captured her fingers and refused the caress. Surely he wasn't going to insist that she begged?

'Goodnight.' He kissed her imprisoned hand and then let her go, disappearing into the darkness. She knew his cabin was situated on the lower terrace beneath hers and wished with all her heart that he had accepted her caress and let her persuade him to stay. What game was he playing? Was he waiting for her to release him from his promise not to touch her, or was he manipulating her emotions until she crawled to his bed, as he had predicted?

The next day Rick took her to Marina del Rey, where he had a cabin cruiser docked. Sleek vessels with brightly coloured sails of all description were tied up or heading out to sea. The sun rather inevitably shone, and the sea was as blue as on a picture postcard. Designer yachting gear shouted wealth; there was none of the practicality that marked Hebridean fishing craft and the men who sailed them.

Rick steered the cruiser out of the arms of the harbour, his body oiled for the sun, a pair of navy shorts with a turquoise stripe down the side his only adornment. Helen had a bright pink bikini on under a voluminous white T-shirt which, despite the breeze, was still too warm, and eventually she relented and stretched out on the deck and let the sun stroke her body. She fancied it was going to be the last holiday she sunned herself on for the following eight months and she might as well make the best of it.

'You'll burn.' Rick sat down beside her when he put the anchor down an hour later and observed her exposed skin. Without another word he began to rub the oil into her back, and Helen's eyes closed in feline bliss.

'Don't you have a home?' she enquired. 'You don't seem the type to live with your mother.'

He paused, mid-action, and then continued, a harder thread entering his voice. 'I've never had anywhere permanent. I've liked to keep on the move. What about you? Have you got a dream house? Something you've always wanted?'

She smiled, peeping over her shoulder at him. 'I didn't think so, until I saw Samhrad Taigh.'

He smiled with what she felt was a certain amount of reluctance. 'That might get a little small if you had a family.'

'Hmm.' She turned away, resting her cheek against her folded hands. Coward, she upbraided herself. Why don't you tell him? He began to work on the backs of her legs and she luxuriated in his touch, which was pleasurable to the point of refined torture. The idea of turning over and letting him continue applying the oil with the evocative massage tantalised her, but it would be an open invitation and she was hesitant about asserting her own sexuality.

'Will you oil my back for me?' Rick handed her the bottle of sun oil and turned on to his stomach, sure of her compliance.

Helen was glad he couldn't see her expression. Pouring the oil on to his back, she began to rub it in, her mouth dry while her spine prickled with perspiration. Green eyes gorged on the strong lines of his body, her fingers gliding over the raised bone of his shoulder-blades and into the sculpted hollows below. His spine made a deep groove down his back, and she followed it to the waistband of his trunks.

'There, you're done.' Her voice held a trace of huskiness, but she was proud of the level of normality she managed to inject.

'Thanks.' He didn't even turn to face her, and she returned to her prone position, thinking of the cool cabin below and the temptation of the double bed.

If the day out was supposed to relax her it had had the opposite effect. The combination of good weather, beautiful surroundings and perfect privacy called mock-

ingly to her senses. When she returned to the Knowleses'
home she was brewing a temper that needed very little
to snap it.

A sense of purpose gripped her as she prepared for
the evening. She answered the knock on the door with
a careless 'come in' as she applied her make-up. Her
dress was still under wraps, but she had showered and
attended to her hair and was dressed in a silken Chinese
wrap of jade-green.

Sylvia Knowles entered with a polite smile. 'Ah,
Helen.' She waved that the younger woman should continue, and sat herself on the edge of the bed. 'I've come
in to apologise.' She gave a small moue of regret as Helen
cast her a glance over her shoulder. 'I've made a little
mistake with the guest list and invited Donna Trevin.'

'Some ex-girlfriend, I take it?' Helen enquired
smoothly.

'She's an actress.' Sylvia sounded piqued that the
Englishwoman had never heard of her. 'She starred in
Only the Children—didn't you see it?'

'I don't go to the cinema very much,' she admitted.
'Was it good?'

'It made a lot of money.' Sylvia gave a faint laugh. 'I
really don't know what to make of you. I don't recognise my own son. He's tense and irritable. It doesn't
appear to be a very satisfactory relationship, you don't
act like lovers——'

'Mrs Knowles,' Helen interrupted quietly, 'I don't
want to be rude, but I think we have to sort this out for
ourselves.'

Sighing, Rick's mother viewed the fair beauty of her
son's fiancée and admitted reluctantly that the girl was
at least straightforward. Donna Trevin might have the
advantage of keeping Rick in the States but she was a
scheming little monster, and with hindsight she regretted
the impulse that had made her issue the invitation.

'I hope you're good at fighting your corner.' Sylvia Knowles went to the door. 'I suppose Donna might stir up the coals a bit. I wouldn't like my son to spend his life hopelessly besotted with some frigid beauty——'

'I think that's very unlikely.' Helen smiled at the thought but the humour didn't last long. When Sylvia Knowles left she stared unhappily into the mirror. Her fear of being vulnerable to the pain her mother had experienced on the death of her husband had made her need cast-iron guarantees before she allowed a man close. She had never explained the way she felt to Rick; instead she had appeared to struggle against the passion that exploded between them and tried to escape from any deeper commitment. Rick's motives remained suspect, but she could hardly expect him to reveal his innermost feelings while she was on the run.

Hearing the music start up, she realised she was late and went to the in-built wardrobe to take out her dress. The panne velvet creation in magenta had a ruched front and full skirt. She wore gold hoop earrings, her throat and upper chest bare, so too her legs, her shoes, high-heeled and peep-toed, matching the dress. Her long gold tresses cascaded over her shoulders, her green eyes made more mysterious by the use of skilful make-up, her mouth painted a voluptuous pink.

Rick was already with a group of friends when she joined the party. He was wearing a stone-coloured suit, with a black polo shirt. He had replenished his tan by the day's sailing, but his eyes when they met hers were as tense as his mother had observed. Helen wondered if she looked the same; she certainly felt as if she were walking the high wire.

'Darling,' he greeted her. 'Come and meet some people. This is Marsha, Devlin, Natasha....' Many of them were well-known faces, but it was when he got to Donna Trevin that she let her gaze rest for a moment.

The other woman eyed her boldly, as if doubting her credentials for the high office she held.

'You must have something special to make Rick propose. I've been working on him for years...'

'In between other assignments,' Rick smoothly intervened, laughing at the dirty look he received.

'He's gone, Donna,' Marsha drawled, wickedly winking at Helen. 'Let it be.'

'"Never say die" is my motto.' Donna was pert. 'He'll come back.' With that she smartly whisked her escort, who was looking bemused, off to the dance-floor.

Helen flicked a glance up at Rick as he cleared his throat and halted the explanation before it began. 'We're both entitled to a past.'

'Nice of you to be so understanding.' He didn't sound as if he thought it was nice at all.

Aware that her temper was perilously fragile, Helen was quite pleased when Devlin O'Connor came up and asked her to dance. On the receiving end of a glowing smile, her partner blinked, but recovered with the speed of a true opportunist. With a quick glance at Rick's stormy countenance he drew her to the other side of the dance-floor.

Devlin O'Connor was the teenage heart-throb of the moment; he was twenty-six and looked eighteen, starring in a host of college and wild-boy movies.

'Never seen the senior hunk jealous before,' he wise-cracked. 'I'm the juvenile hunk, filthy rich and with no aspirations to be an ac-tor.'

Helen couldn't help smiling. 'Is that an advantage?'

'It certainly is. I don't worry about quality, just the size of the cheque. It gives life a certain simplicity.'

'It must,' she agreed. 'I don't think Rick is pretentious about what he does; I just think he has to get involved or he'd be bored.'

Devlin grinned. 'He's OK. One of the few that don't get snowed under by the hype. I wouldn't mind pinching you off him, though; I just adore English voices, and yours is as cool as an after-dinner mint.'

Helen glanced over at Rick, to find he had disappeared. Searching the dance-floor, she stiffened slightly as she saw him with the raven-haired Donna, who had draped herself around him. The blood roared through her veins and she gritted her teeth to stop herself marching across the floor and dragging them apart. The music seemed to stay in a melancholic or seductive vein, giving Donna Trevin licence to flaunt her body brazenly.

'I think you should throw Donna into the pool,' Devlin suggested wickedly, noting the direction of her gaze. 'It would help her cool down.'

'Champagne has so much more style,' she murmured, picking up two glasses as a waiter passed and leaving Devlin O'Connor standing with an incredulous look that turned into a smile as she approached the entwined pair.

Rick flashed a dark glance in her direction and, seeing the glint in her eyes, made an attempt to free himself, but Donna was as persistent as a leech.

'Champagne for two,' she announced herself grimly. The stumble she affected was barely plausible and certainly didn't fool either of her victims. She had the pleasure of showering Rick in the fizzy liquid and pouring the other glass down Donna's cleavage as they broke apart.

Another headline, she thought, a little light-headed, but at least that one I'll deserve.

Donna was not amused, and Rick dragged her back as she attempted to vent her spleen on her adversary. His eyes promised retribution and Helen was already backing off when he handed the distraught actress over to the woman called Marsha and began purposefully to stalk her.

Sylvia Knowles had come late on to the scene but interpreted it quickly. 'Rick...' she inserted herself in between the couple, putting her hand up to her son's chest '...I'm sure it was an accident. Helen didn't mean to——'

'I did!' Helen was unrepentant.

'Dear, you're not helping. He's got a filthy temper and I doubt you can outrun him.'

'Why not?' Rick took his mother by the shoulders and moved her sideways. 'She's had plenty of practice. She's an emotional escape artist.'

The party appeared to be continuing, with centres of attention either on their small cluster or Donna, who was, no doubt, swearing revenge. Taking a few steps backwards, Helen kicked off her shoes and ran across the stone flag towards the cabin she had been given. The terrace system slowed her down, and she responded in panic to the sound of footsteps behind her. Turning, she grabbed Rick's arms as he caught hold of her, struggling wildly as he picked her up and ignored her cabin, striding relentlessly towards his own.

'I'm not sleeping with you,' she spat at him as he put her down to open the door.

'It isn't sleeping I want you for,' he remarked with blunt crudity, keeping hold of a swath of her hair as she tried to get away, impervious to her cry of protest.

'I'm sure your friend Donna would oblige,' she sniped bitchily.

'I'm sure she would.' Rick bundled her in the door with as much force as it took, regarding her hostility, as she rubbed her arms, with brutal indifference. 'But I have a craving for something golden and cool with a red-hot centre that's driving me absolutely crazy. I don't know what to do any more. I try to lay off to give you time and you torture me with those simmering looks you specialise in.' Taking off his damp jacket, he raked his fingers through his hair, grimacing at the faint stickiness, and looked at her, shaking his head. 'Then you do something like this because I dance with another woman...'

'You weren't dancing—it was obscene...' Her green eyes were livid. 'And you did it on purpose, which is worse!'

'Why would I do that?' He pretended patience while his gaze challenged her and his jaw flexed tensely.

'Because you wanted me to...' She broke off, hugging herself with her arms and turned away.

'What?' He pulled her back round, refusing to let her hide.

'You wanted me to claim you,' she shouted at him, unaware of the hunted, scared look she couldn't hide.

'Damn right!' he agreed, his hands warm against her naked shoulders. 'I've chased you like some lovesick fool since the moment I set eyes on you. After we made love that first time I was so scared you'd go back to London and get walked over by Burton. You seemed so vulnerable. I thought you were fighting your conscience over starting an affair with a married man. When we made love it seemed logical that it was your inexperience that was stopping you, and once I'd shown you how good it could be——'

'Michael Burton?' she repeated incredulously. 'The only thing I felt about him was guilt that I might have, in some way, encouraged him. If he were the last man on earth I'd take a vow of celibacy.'

Rick regarded her steadily. 'What if I were the last man on earth? What then?'

Helen's fingers intertwined and she swallowed drily. 'I'd have to fight off the other women.'

It wasn't what he wanted, and she could see the frustration darken his eyes. Why was it so hard to say what she wanted to... to admit how much he meant to her?

'I know it's locked in here somewhere.' His fingers drew a line from just below her ear to the neckline of her dress. 'Mingled with that fire and jealousy, I know some small part of you cares about me.' Tipping up her chin, he kissed the begging curve of her mouth, feeding the hunger in her. Drawing back, he observed the regret and kindled desire with satisfaction.

'Going to name the day?' His hands were warm on her shoulders, pushing under the cascade of golden hair. Her eyes narrowed but he could tell she had registered the question, even though the shiver that greeted his teasing stroke of her nape seemed to suggest that her attention was elsewhere.

'Tomorrow, the next day,' she whispered, wanting the touching to go on, 'whenever you want.'

'We finally communicate.' He smiled into her eyes. 'Now, repeat after me...' his lips brushed hers '...I...love...you.'

'I—er—love you.' Hers was quick and hurried, and he viewed her with mock criticism.

'"I—er—love you" will do for now. See if this makes it any easier.' His mouth ceased its teasing and moved over hers possessively, his hard, firm lips worrying the soft tremble of hers, coaxing them apart and feeling the urgency in her body as she pressed her slim, curvaceous form against the hard muscle and bone of his.

They were desperate for each other, the problems in their relationship enforcing a sensual desert that had tortured them with physical cravings. Helen's head fell back as his mouth plundered the hollows of her shoulders and collar-bone, feeling his hot breath and his teeth graze against the pulse in her throat. Her hands buried under his black polo shirt, baring his midriff with its line of body hair, her fingers following it to the waistband of his trousers.

'Oh, Helen,' he groaned, burying his face against the
curve of her breast. His hands smoothed the velvet over
her hips, pulling her against him, his head lifting, his
eyes blazing with emotion. 'You're all the woman I'll
ever want. I just hope in time you'll learn to trust me.
I hate to see you look scared and lost; it cuts me up to
think I do that to you.'

'You don't. Not any more.' She took his hand and
tugged him towards the bedroom, mischief in her eyes
as well as sexual intent. 'I have something to tell you,
but I think it can wait a little while.'

'I think it had better.' He kissed her neck as she turned
for him to undo her zip, his hands sweeping around to
curve over her breasts when the magenta velvet loosened
under his persuasion. 'You're beautiful.' His voice
sounded ragged. 'I've never wanted a woman so much.'

Helen turned in his arms, coaxing him to take his shirt
off and running her hands lightly up his chest, admiring
the muscular build, the small, flat male nipples buried
in a shadow of hair. Turning her exploration into a
kissing one, she let her tongue rub leisurely against his
salty skin, her female nature flaring into full bloom as
his urgency made him rough with her dress. She wanted
his possession, wanted those strong brown hands to
mould her body, wanted to hold the strength of his body
in her own and exhaust him in the timeless dance of
passion. She must have whispered to him because he
obeyed her need, stripping her naked and throwing off
his own clothes so that he could pull her bare flesh
against his.

She backed on to the bed, moving across so that he
could join her, her green eyes luminous and bewitching,
her hand reaching out to stroke his thigh, only too aware
of the male potency of his body.

His tongue stroked her lips apart, her white teeth
parting on a kittenish sound of passion as his fingers

worked their magic on her body. Languidly he probed the edge of her teeth, feeling her thighs quiver as he made her ready for him, her womanly loins becoming moist and giving. She wanted more than this teasing pressure, and his body grew hot and hard at the sounds he was muffling with his mouth. Her nails scored his back and he moved over her, his hip-bone pressing into her, one hand hooking under her knee, his mouth sealing hers and engaging her tongue in a brazen duel as he pressed against her.

Helen tangled her fingers in his hair, welcoming the male encroachment, her guttural moan greeting the surge of the male force into her body, static screaming over her skin as he penetrated her silken sheath.

'I love you.' She searched blindly for his mouth when he moved his lips to her ear. 'Rick, I love you.'

Placing desperate kisses over her face, Rick soothed her hot, dry lips before swooping to the temptation of her arched body and the golden slope of her breast. His hands ran from under her arms to the length of her thighs, pushing under her buttocks and bringing her up to meet the vital thrusts of his body.

Their passion tore down any remaining defences, white-hot flame curling through their bodies, burning out the weaker emotions until only love remained supreme.

Later, when they rested in the after-glow of love, she told him about the effect her father's death had had on both Moira Howard and herself.

'I thought I could make myself safe if I didn't care,' she admitted reluctantly. 'Then that became pointless because I realised, when you went out to search for Andy in the helicopter, that the agony of losing you would be just the same whether I admitted I loved you or not. You had never said you loved me,' she pointed out in her own defence.

'I couldn't keep away from you,' he growled, his mouth curling with amusement. 'I played every low-down trick in the book to keep you from taking off. Every time I thought I'd got you you seemed to find some way to escape. I wanted you to be pregnant so it would give me an excuse to whisk you to the altar. After we made love you were so damn sexy that I couldn't bear to let you loose on the male half of the population. The transition was painfully obvious when I watched those tapes of your programme. Then you were all innocent promise.' The glow from the bedside lamp showed the blue lights in his eyes with flecks of green against a background of gold. He was relaxed and happier than she had seen him for weeks.

'About being pregnant…' She began feeling the sudden focus of attention on her face.

'Yes,' he agreed patiently.

Taking a deep breath, she plunged into an explanation that was halted by his low, silent laughter.

'You knew!' She punched him in the ribs, her eyes militant.

'I guessed you'd lied; you didn't look very convincing when you suddenly denied you were having a baby.'

Realising that he had put up with rather a lot from her, she subsided, and he raised a mocking eyebrow.

'Anything else?'

'Yes, you can tell that Trevin woman that you are no longer available. If she comes near you again she'll have more than champagne to worry about.'

'I don't think anyone will be in any doubt about the way I feel.' He lay back in the bed, his finger stroking around her jaw as she leaned over him, his gaze absorbed with her. 'We'll make our home on Cladach, but this is part of my life too. That's why I brought you here. There are people like Donna and Michael Burton everywhere, but they can't touch us now. There's strong magic between us two; I told you that, don't you remember?'

She did, and her eyes lit with laughter. 'You were chatting me up.'

'I was planning to island-hop until I found you. It was a little disconcerting finding you on Cladach. It still is.'

'Does it bother you?' She turned her head slightly, gently biting the finger that had travelled to the side of her mouth.

'I think I can live with it,' he murmured, gathering her up in his arms and turning her under him, prepared to demonstrate just how much she bothered him and just exactly how he was prepared to cope.

EPILOGUE

THE midsummer ceilidh once again saluted the sun's journey to its furthest northern point. The Frazer family was complete that day, James and his bride having flown in from Los Angeles to spend their honeymoon in their island home.

The family had a lot to celebrate, Helen reflected, tucking a light blanket around her small daughter, Jade Fiona Frazer. Sarah and Andy's little girl, Janet, would have her first birthday the next day. She was a happy little toddler, thoroughly intrigued by her three-month-old cousin, who would join in the birthday celebrations with a similar lack of comprehension.

Sarah had remained remarkably uncritical during the first stage of the hotel's development. Maybe it was Sarah's way of showing her gratitude for the help she had been given. It was hard to tell; nothing was ever said. James's departure had left ample scope for his sister to develop her management skills, and she had taken to it like a duck to water. It had been decided that much of the land would be classed as a nature reserve, with clearly defined restrictions on use and access. Not that there weren't occasional clashes between Sarah and her more volatile brother. Helen and Andy had become skilled negotiators and managed to avoid any of the rifts becoming yawning chasms.

'And where is Daddy?' Helen crooned to her baby daughter. 'Up to his eyes in concrete, do you think?'

'No, I've stopped building hotels for today.' A drily amused voice came from the doorway and Helen jumped, turning to view Rick's tall figure, leaning against the door-jamb.

'You gave me a shock!' she whispered in reproof, dancing lights in her eyes showing she forgave him. He came to stand beside her and looked down at their small daughter.

'You shouldn't talk about me behind my back.' He leant over, stroking the baby's chubby cheek. Jade had tufts of dark hair and huge green eyes. She chuckled winsomely and quite clearly melted her father's heart. 'Have I been neglecting you?' He raised a dark eyebrow, smiling, but there was a question in his eyes.

'Well, no...I know you can't help it,' she reassured him, referring to his various projects and hobbies, labelled 'obsessions' when she was in a less benevolent mood.

Amused, he tilted her chin. 'I wasn't aware of any lack of interest...' Kissing her, he eased back to see the dreamy look in her green eyes.

'That isn't what I meant.' Linking her arms around his neck, she regarded him with deep tenderness. 'It doesn't matter.'

Frowning, he sighed. 'You won't be interested, then.'

'What?' She tugged his hair, annoyed by his teasing.

'Well, I was toying with the idea of doing a series of TV programmes covering the history of the islands. We could do flora, fauna, and all the historical bits too. I could direct and do some of the interviews, and you could do the rest. What do you think?'

She thought it was a wonderful idea. Her eyes shone with enthusiasm. It would allow them to work together and have Jade with them too.

'I love you,' she breathed against his lips before she kissed him, and was getting quite carried away with her gratitude when a hearty knock on the door announced Andy's presence.

'They're about to make the speeches. Rick, are you to say a few words?'

'I sincerely hope not,' he murmured, receiving a chiding look from his wife.

'He's shy,' she explained to Andy, who chuckled at the thought.

It was Sarah who surprised them all. After James had made the annual speech, welcoming the guests to the ceilidh, Sarah announced that she would like to make a special toast. She spoke of the dilemma of island life in the twentieth century and for a moment seemed to be on her old soap box.

'But new things...' she glanced at Helen and Rick and smiled '...aren't always bad things. It's something that's taken me a long time to learn. This year has brought us two weddings and two babies. It's also brought a new and very dear friend to the island. I hope Helen will accept this as a way of saying "thank you" from me, and "welcome home" from every islander here today.'

The gift was a golden medallion. On it was the emblem of the eagle and thistle. Every islander received one as a christening present, and Helen felt her eyes mist and a lump come into her throat at the message it implied. Everyone raised their glasses in a toast. Lifting damp eyelashes first to Rick and then to acknowledge her family and friends, Helen felt surrounded by love and happiness, a silent thank-you going to Fiona MacSween, who had taught her the names of the islands as a childhood rhyme and left her an inheritance of joy.

Next Month's Romances

Each month you can choose from a world of variety in romance with Mills & Boon. Below are the new titles to look out for next month, why not ask either Mills & Boon Reader Service or your Newsagent to reserve you a copy of the titles you want to buy — just tick the titles you would like to order and either post to Reader Service or take it to any Newsagent and ask them to order your books.

Please save me the following titles:	Please tick	√
STORMFIRE	Helen Bianchin	
LAW OF ATTRACTION	Penny Jordan	
DANGEROUS SANCTUARY	Anne Mather	
ROMANTIC ENCOUNTER	Betty Neels	
A DARING PROPOSITION	Miranda Lee	
NO PROVOCATION	Sophie Weston	
LAST OF THE GREAT FRENCH LOVERS	Sarah Holland	
CAVE OF FIRE	Rebecca King	
NO MISTRESS BUT LOVE	Kate Proctor	
INTRIGUE	Margaret Mayo	
ONE LOVE FOREVER	Barbara McMahon	
DOUBLE FIRE	Mary Lyons	
STONE ANGEL	Helen Brooks	
THE ORCHARD KING	Miriam Macgregor	
LAW OF THE CIRCLE	Rosalie Ash	
THE HOUSE ON CHARTRES STREET	Rosemary Hammond	

If you would like to order these books from Mills & Boon Reader Service please send £1.70 per title to: Mills & Boon Reader Service, P.O. Box 236, Croydon, Surrey, CR9 3RU and quote your Subscriber No:..(If applicable) and complete the name and address details below. Alternatively, these books are available from many local Newsagents including W.H.Smith, J.Menzies, Martins and other paperback stockists from 6th July 1992.

Name:..

Address:..

....Post Code:.......................

To Retailer: If you would like to stock M&B books please contact your regular book/magazine wholesaler for details.

You may be mailed with offers from other reputable companies as a result of this application. If you would rather not take advantage of these opportunities please tick box ☐

4 FREE

Romances
and 2 FREE gifts
just for you!

You can enjoy all the
heartwarming emotion of true love for FREE!
Discover the heartbreak and the happiness, the emotion and
the tenderness of the modern relationships in
Mills & Boon Romances.

We'll send you 4 captivating Romances as a special offer from
Mills & Boon Reader Service, along with the chance to have
6 Romances delivered to your door each month.

Claim your FREE books and gifts overleaf...

An irresistible offer from Mills & Boon

Here's a personal invitation from Mills & Boon Reader Service, to become a regular reader of Romances. To welcome you, we'd like you to have 4 books, a CUDDLY TEDDY and a special MYSTERY GIFT absolutely FREE.

Then you could look forward each month to receiving 6 brand new Romances, delivered to your door, postage and packing free! Plus our free Newsletter featuring author news, competitions, special offers and much more.

This invitation comes with no strings attached. You may cancel or suspend your subscription at any time, and still keep your free books and gifts.

It's so easy. Send no money now. Simply fill in the coupon below and post it to -
Reader Service, FREEPOST, PO Box 236, Croydon, Surrey CR9 9EL.

- - - - - - - - - - **NO STAMP REQUIRED** - - - - - - - - - -

Free Books Coupon

Yes! Please rush me 4 free Romances and 2 free gifts! Please also reserve me a Reader Service subscription. If I decide to subscribe I can look forward to receiving 6 brand new Romances each month for just £10.20, postage and packing free. If I choose not to subscribe I shall write to you within 10 days - I can keep the books and gifts whatever I decide. I may cancel or suspend my subscription at any time. I am over 18 years of age.

Ms/Mrs/Miss/Mr _____ EP31R

Address _____

_____

Postcode _____ Signature _____